"Your little experiment seems to have worked."

Leone laughed lightly and, she hoped, condescendingly. "I'm feeling much less tense now."

"Good," Gray said sarcastically, guiding the car through the wide gates of her home. "It should save you a pound or two on psychiatric advice."

Leone clenched her teeth. "I don't think I was in *that* much of a state. But at least it proved one thing—that you would *not* make a satisfactory substitute for Simon. So I'll just have to put up with my... sexual frustration, I think you called it, till I can get Simon to the altar."

"Really." He leaned across her to unlock the door. She recoiled and he laughed softly. "If you think that's going to cure you ... think again!"

Alexandra Scott was born in a small Scottish village. She married an English soldier, and their travels, which took them to the Far East and various parts of Europe, proved to be good preparation for her later career as a writer. She had always wanted to write a book but was reluctant to actually try until she and her husband eventually settled in Yorkshire and he signed her up for a writers' course. She still has that wonderful, exciting feeling each time one of her books is accepted.

Books by Alexandra Scott

HARLEQUIN ROMANCE
2506—LOVE ME AGAIN
2514—THIS SIDE OF HEAVEN
2554—CATCH A STAR
2585—LOVE COMES STEALING
2604—BORROWED GIRL
2663—STORM WARNING

These books may be available at your local bookseller.

Don't miss any of our special offers. Write to us at the following address for information on our newest releases.

Harlequin Reader Service
901 Fuhrmann Blvd., P.O. Box 1325, Buffalo, NY 14269
Canadian address: P.O. Box 2800, Postal Station A,
5170 Yonge St., Willowdale, Ont. M2N 6J3

Wildfire

Alexandra Scott

Harlequin Books

TORONTO • NEW YORK • LONDON
AMSTERDAM • PARIS • SYDNEY • HAMBURG
STOCKHOLM • ATHENS • TOKYO • MILAN

Original hardcover edition published in 1985
by Mills & Boon Limited

ISBN 0-373-02769-9

Harlequin Romance first edition June 1986

CHAPTER ONE

WITH a murmur that might have been anything Leone turned away from her mother's brimming eyes, from her trembling expressions of sympathy and, running now, urgent in her desire for privacy, she took the steps of the curving staircase two at a time. A few long strides took her into the room which she had known from childhood, but today she saw nothing of its familiar layout, sparing not the briefest of glances for the billowing tissue-shrouded bundle supported by a velvet-covered clothes hanger, hooked over the top of the mahogany wardrobe.

Collapsing on to the stool in front of the dressing-table she stared into densely violet eyes, wondering with blank amazement that she looked very much as usual. And yet ... for just a moment she leaned forward towards the glass, her cheek supported by pink-tipped fingers, but the lines of strain and shock which she thought had flickered for a moment about her features were not in evidence.

She groaned, her expression instantly disfigured by a frown of self-disgust. What kind of person was she? She shook her head in total disbelief. For heaven's sake! On Saturday she was to have been married with all the show that might have been expected for the only child of Sir Piers Chevenix, even now workmen were tapping in the last peg which would secure the enormous marquee in the grounds, the choirboys she imagined would be practising hard, perhaps not arrayed in blue surplices and white frills but nevertheless practising hard to reach the perfection which the occasion would demand, and all oblivious of the fact that the wedding would not take place.

She could imagine the despair and disappointment which would affect so many, guests, caterers, photographers, the families of both bride and groom who had been so wildly thrilled that the friendship of more than thirty years was to be cemented by the splendid ceremony on Saturday. But now, car hire firms would miss out on many casual trips, British Rail . . . a flicker of hysteria rose inside her as she tried to recall the numbers who had planned to arrive by first-class pullman coach . . .

For a few seconds she imagined the entire British economy being brought to its knees and that was the moment when Leone, by making a supreme effort, got her imagination under control. Weddings had been cancelled before, guests had been disappointed and the world had not ended as a result.

But what in this case was more of a problem was that the bride, surely the person in the whole wild extravaganza who was most entitled to feel disappointment, and disappointment verging on despair, could only thank God that her prayers had been answered and that she had been saved from the consequences of her own weakness. Poor Simon, of course she was sorry, sorry and bitterly upset for him, so she told herself repeatedly, but her own feelings of relief and release kept forcing aside those which would have been far more seemly

'Darling.' There was the briefest of knocks on the door of her bedroom before it opened and her mother poked her head inside. 'I've brought you some tea.' With the heel of an elegant grey shoe she pushed the door closed and advanced into the room with her tray which she held with the awkwardness of a prize fighter in a ballet class. Lady Chevenix was used to having servants perform the lightest of tasks but clearly this was an exceptional circumstance. 'There.' Leone could see that the tray placed on a small table close to the window held two cups and saucers as well as teapot. 'Now come on, Leone,' briskness was not in Lady Chevenix's nature but this was a time when extreme measures were needed, 'I know you have had a terrible shock but you'll feel better when you've had a hot drink.'

'Thanks, Mum.' Leone forgot how much her mother hated this form of address but for once it was not remarked on. She rose from her seat in front of the dressing-table, took one of the chairs drawn up by the table. 'A cup of tea is just what I want.' Unseeingly her eyes took in the small lake at the far side of the park, richly draped with majestic willows, as she stirred the cup which had been put in her hand.

'Now,' having at least in her own opinion, provided her daughter with some alleviation for her broken heart, Lady Chevenix felt entitled to look at her through the blur of tears, 'don't mind me, Leone.' Her voice trembled, she choked over her teacup. 'If you want to cry, then do.'

'I don't want to cry, Mother.' Shaming as it was to admit, still she knew she could depend on a wrong interpretation being put on the words.

'There, I knew.' Lady Chevenix found a wisp of lace in her sleeve, dabbed it at her eyes. 'You're suffering from shock. And you never have been a weepy sort of child.'

Leone sipped at the sweet tea without answering although it did occur to her that she had hardly, over the twenty-five years of her life, had anything to cry over. She was feeling even more guilty about her mother's tears than the lack of her own but still she could think of nothing to say. Lady Chevenix gave a shuddering sigh and put her handkerchief away.

'I managed to contact your father at the golf club, darling. He'll be back straight away.'

'What did he say?'

'Oh, he's stunned of course. And worried for you, Leone. Don't,' in a gesture of commiseration she leaned forward to touch her daughter's hand, 'don't hide your feelings *too* much, will you, dear? It isn't good to bottle up your emotions.'

'No, I won't, Mother.' Her smile was as wan as any mother could have wished and Lady Chevenix succumbed to another gush of tears. 'I'm sorry, it's going to be so much for you and Daddy.' She shrugged rather aimlessly. 'Having to cancel everything. And after so much preparation.'

'Yes.' The older woman sniffed. 'It's going to be a Herculean task but . . .'

'. . . But,' Leone tried to be cheerful, 'weddings have been cancelled before now. It will only be a nine days' wonder.'

'Not cancelled, Leone. Postponed. Just as soon as Simon has recovered from this accident we'll set the whole thing in motion again. Don't worry about that.' She rose, replaced the things on the tray and walked with it to the door. 'Then . . . I'd better go and start telephoning around.'

'Would you like me to come and help you, Mother?'

'No, not unless you feel you must, darling. If I were in your situation the last thing I could bear doing would be explaining to people what has happened. And the last thing we want is for you to be any more upset than you are now.'

Leone, who felt she was not playing her part with the drama demanded by the circumstances, tried to reorganise her features. 'Then, if you don't mind . . .'

'Of course I don't. Besides, Piers said he would stop at the office and pick up Miss Drury.' Pausing by the wardrobe and the heavily protected wedding dress Lady Chevenix sighed deeply. 'When I think that you won't be wearing your gorgeous dress on Saturday, I could cry.' A few instant tears were shed. 'But we must think of the positive side,' she admonished herself, including her daughter in a watery smile, 'after all, what do a few weeks matter when you have an entire lifetime . . . And so long as dear Simon is all right in the end.'

When finally the door had closed Leone stood staring at its white glossy surface for a few dazed moments before allowing all her guilt and remorse to rise up and swallow her. They were feelings she was unused to and the new experience was not one she was enjoying. Only she sensed she'd better get used to them and quickly, for this was merely a reprieve.

Her mother's words had made that abundantly clear. Now she was faced with the certainty that the wedding which everyone else would look on as postponed for a few weeks because of the bridegroom's unfortunate traffic accident was, as far as the bride was concerned, cancelled, nullified and repudiated. It was as dead as the Dodo and should never have been thought of in the first place.

Leone twisted the huge diamond round her finger and wondered how she could have got herself into such a mess. As if she didn't know. It had been an unholy combination of sentimentality and champagne, a devilish alliance if ever there was one. That and a straightforward misunderstanding on Simon's part. He, too, had probably been suffering the effects of the same brew which had caused him to take maybe for yes. And then to compound his error by blurting out the news the moment Anita and David had left for their honeymoon after their Easter wedding! And the besotted delight shown by all concerned robbed Leone of the courage to correct the situation when she regained her right mind again.

Besides, there had been that tiny stab of envy when she had seen Anita drive off with David, she had been holding his hand and looking up into his face as if he were the moon and the sun and not just ordinary David Shedden at all. A pang which reminded her that although she was two years older than her best friend, she still had no idea just what that feeling was like. Not that she was really envious, of course, she was too fond of both to begrudge them a moment of their happiness. But to think, all those times they had gone round in a foursome, assuring each other that it was merely for convenience and insisting that each was free to make other arrangements when it suited, swearing total emotional freedom.

That was what made it all the more stunning when, at the beginning of March, Anita announced that she and David were to be married at Easter.

'Easter? David?' Leone was sure her jaw must have dropped. 'But *Easter*, that's only a month's time.'

'I know.' Anita had blushed a little. 'But suddenly I know that I can't wait. And David feels the same. You know he's thirty-eight and there's Davey, so there's no reason why we should.'

'Of course I *do* see that.' What else was there to say? Besides, it was obvious enough that there was a great deal of sense in what Anita had said. David Shedden was a widower with a five-year-old son and so there was no point in delay.

'And Easter.' Anita was so positively dreamy that Leone felt her first painful little stab just then, but of course it could not be jealousy. 'I've always wanted to be married then and of course I'm hoping you'll be my bridesmaid, love.'

'Of course I will.' Leone smiled. 'I was taking that for granted. But I'm just a bit bowled over by the news. You and David and all that nonsense about not getting involved . . .'

'But I meant it. Of course I meant it.' Her tone was so vehement that she could only have been telling the truth. Faint colour crept across her cheeks again. 'Then suddenly, it was just about New Year, you remember that party you couldn't go to because you were going out with Chris Ashton, I think that was when it happened. Wham, bang and I was in love.'

And that probably had been at the back of Leone's mind when Simon had proposed to her at the wedding reception. What had happened to Anita could possibly, no probably, happen to her. She liked Simon so much and the idea was bound to grow on her. There was everything to be said for it after all, the lifelong friendship between both sets of parents and the essential fact that she was in love with no one else. Never had been. Once or twice moonlight and tender music had inclined her to think she might . . . but at last she began to suspect that she was expecting too much. Maybe what she felt for Simon *was* love and if that was the case then marriage between them was what it was all about. But as the preparations moved ahead with the inevitability of a juggernaut she became more and more conscious of being caught in a trap, one which she herself had sprung.

It was then that more in hope than expectation she began to pray. And this, she supposed, was the answer to those prayers. She crossed her fingers and raised her eyes ceilingwards in an attempt to show gratitude for the response to her desperate appeal then felt a pang of conscience. Poor Simon, it was a bit hard on him but maybe, in the long run, it would be best for him too . . .

Not that he would be thinking that right now. Well, right now, she glanced at her tiny diamond studded watch, he might just be coming round from the anaesthetic, but when he had time to think what the accident meant, he would be distraught. And not solely on account of their elaborate arrangements. For Leone had no doubt that Simon loved her. Although he had taken so long to inform her he had been in love with her for years. Quite frankly he was crazy about her and there had been times over the last few months when Leone had wondered if that was part of the trouble. If she had been a little less certain of his undying devotion would she possibly have found him more attractive?

Not that he was unattractive, in fact he was quite good-looking. There were plenty of girls in the area who would have been only too happy to find themselves the object of Simon Darcy's attention and not just because his family was one of the wealthiest in the area, he was quite good fun and handsome in a conventional sort of way. Tall, dark and handsome . . . well yes. Only when you're five feet seven yourself then five feet nine isn't exactly exalted and when your own hair is black as pitch then dark brown is simply mouse, and handsome, well she already had her own thoughts on that.

Leone caught sight of herself in the mirror and blushed scarlet at her unworthy reflections of the man she had been within hours of promising to love and honour until death. What a mean spoiled little brat she must be. Simon was always so kind, so understanding, so utterly . . . utterly . . . The word for which her mind was searching evaded her completely and when she heard someone knocking on the door her answer showed some irritation.

'Sorry.' Her father's head poked round the door. 'Just say if you'd rather I went and left you alone.'

'Oh, Daddy.' For the first time she felt herself dangerously close to tears. 'Of course not. Come on in.'

'Well,' Sir Piers made no attempt to touch her but stood in the centre of the room regarding her through eyes which once had the brilliance of her own but which now had faded a little, 'this is a shock for everyone isn't it, pet?'

'Yes.' The endearment, a hangover from childhood, slipped out, obliging Leone to bite her lower lip with some force before she could continue. 'Shock is an understatement. Poor Simon.'

'You've heard how he is?'

'Mmmm.' She nodded to give herself an extra second. 'After his mother rang with the news of the accident I called the hospital. They said he was as well as could be expected, just what they always say, that he was in the theatre having his leg set and that it would be best if I didn't go down till this evening.'

'Did you tell them? About the wedding plans I mean?'

'No.' Leone shook her head, the dark silky hair swaying about her lowered face. 'I can't think now why I didn't.' Deep down she suspected she was afraid of the hospital authorities being so sympathetic that they would suggest getting Simon to church on a stretcher if necessary. 'I suppose I wasn't thinking clearly.'

'I don't suppose there's any chance . . .'

'No, none.' She interrupted a shade too quickly then wondered if her relief had shown through. She hurried on. 'They did say it was a complex break and he has other injuries as well, minor ones they said. So I can see no way Simon is going to feel the least bit like going through all that performance on Saturday, can you, Daddy?' She raised her head and at once wished she had not, as his intent expression took in every detail of her face.

'No, I suppose not.' He spoke slowly and she had the impression, as she had had once or twice over the past weeks, that perhaps her father too had one or two reservations about her engagement. 'Besides,' he gave a tiny shrug and a laugh, 'what bride is going to welcome a wedding procession with a gorgon of a nurse pushing the bridegroom in a wheelchair?'

'Oh,' again she found herself biting her lips, 'do I sound as if that's all I'm thinking about?'

'Of course not.' Now he came close enough to put an arm about her shoulders and hug her. 'In any case you would be a strange bride if you weren't concerned with all these things. I know how important they are to a girl. It's just a pity your mother went quite so mad with all the preparations, it means such a task putting everything into cold store.'

'I suppose I ought to go down and lend a hand.' Leone sniffed and accepted the large handkerchief which was thrust towards her. 'Did you bring Miss Drury with you?'

He nodded. 'I should leave them to it. Too many people complicate matters still further. You are going to see Simon later on?'

'Yes. I asked when I could go in and they said any time after seven this evening.'

'Want me to run you in?'

'No.' A swift shake of the head. 'Thanks, Daddy. I'll be all right. I imagine his parents will be there and they'll probably let us stay only a few minutes. And poor Simon won't feel like speaking in any case.'

'Probably not. Well, if that's how you prefer it . . . But if you do want to change your mind remember, I'll be on call.'

'Thank you.' There was no reason why the tears should have begun to flow in earnest just then, but they did. 'Oh, Daddy.' And it was amazingly comforting to feel the strength of his arms about her.

The visit to the hospital was much as she had thought it would be. Simon's parents were there long before Leone and surely it was her imagination, her guilty imagination, that put a reproachful expression in Mrs Darcy's eyes? Or possibly it was only disappointment she saw there when she straightened up after brushing her lips against Simon's.

'Is he . . . Did they say when they expected him to recover consciousness?'

'No.' From Mr Darcy whose faint smile was genuinely sympathetic. 'They've said very little.'

'If you had been here a moment earlier, Leone. He did come round for just a second.' Mrs Darcy bit her lip, tightened her possessive grip on the hand of her only child. 'And he said something, I'm sure it was your name.'

'Oh.' Guilt ravaged her emotions so she couldn't look across the hump of bedclothes. 'They . . . they said there was no point in coming till after seven.'

'That's what they told us, too, but I couldn't just sit at home. I *had* to come and find out how he was.' Implicit in her remark was the suggestion that his bride might have been expected to feel a similar urgency.

'Well,' Mr Darcy held out a hand and touched the girl whom his son was expected to marry, 'it's been a shock for all of us. I suppose your mother is in a tailspin cancelling all the arrangements.'

Before Leone could reply Mrs Darcy butted in. 'I should have thought it was a bit early for that.'

'Do you think,' Leone faced the older woman more

courageously, 'Simon is going to be fit for a wedding on Saturday? Just two days from now?'

'Well . . . no. I suppose it's unlikely. But who's to say what he'll be like when the effects of the drugs wear off?'

'Well,' Leone heard her voice sounding all quavery but could do little to strengthen it, 'I can't see it.' Looking at the still figure on the bed, his face, apart from the darkness about his chin, as white as chalk and covers hardly disturbed by his breathing, she was suddenly assailed by doubts of the most frightening kind. Suppose, just suppose the doctors had not been telling the truth, suppose his injuries were much worse than they were admitting, his appearance gave every encouragement to such thoughts. Suppose . . . the still figure looked so little like the man she knew, that all kinds of nightmarish possibilities filled her mind. And it had all come about by her desperation to escape from the results of her own stupidity . . . Reality began to spin away from her and . . .

Then, as if from a great distance she heard Mr Darcy speaking in an agitated voice, he was telling her to sit down, forcing her into a chair and pushing her head between her knees. And gradually she found her senses returning, she looked up into the quietly understanding face with a vague, apologetic smile.

'I'm so sorry. For a moment I felt quite giddy.'

'Are you trying to frighten the life out of me, young woman? Look, I'm going to take you along for a cup of tea. Meggy, you'll be all right on your own for a bit. It doesn't look as if Simon will wake just yet but if he does then you can run along to the waiting room and tell us.'

And the next thing she knew Leone was being led along the corridor towards the waiting room where the

Red Cross ran a small shop and provided drinks for the benefit of patients and staff. The set-up was a familiar one to Leone as she served on the rota as an assistant, it being one of the many voluntary jobs taken on by Lady Chevenix in a fit of enthusiasm which had quickly faded and which Leone had inherited.

She sat in the corner of the waiting room, out of sight of the people behind the counter whom she might know and who might be inclined to ask questions, looking up with a grateful smile as Mr Darcy placed the cup of tea on the table in front of her.

'Sweet. Is that all right?'

'Perfectly.' For the first time she managed a genuine smile. 'I don't as a rule. Take sugar I mean. But they do say it's good for shock, don't they?'

'Oh I'm sorry, Leone.' His face was concerned. 'Of course. I ought to have remembered.'

'Never mind. Even my own mother forgot today so you have an excuse.'

'Well, Enid ... She probably had the right idea about providing something for shock. I just wasn't thinking I'm afraid. I ...'

'Do you know exactly what happened, Uncle Darcy?' It was so many years since she had used that name that both of them, surprised, smiled wanly at each other. She sipped slowly, unexpectedly enjoying the tea heavily spiked with sugar.

'Yes.' All at once his face was grim. 'The police came round to the office to tell me. Of course, they all know Simon well enough and thought it best to contact me rather than going up to the house and possibly finding Meggy on her own. It might easily have been so much worse, my dear.'

'Oh?' The violet eyes were wide in her shocked face, guilt stabbed again as she thought of her own responsibility. If she had prayed less fervently . . . Mr Darcy was continuing.

'It was a gravel lorry coming down Piper's Hill. There was a brake failure and . . .'

'Oh no.' It was hardly even a whisper, more a recognition of the full horror of what might have happened. Piper's Hill was a well-known accident black spot in the small Dorset town where they lived and with a newly opened quarry high above Heyport, it was becoming even more of a hazard.

'Yes. Fortunately the lorry driver wasn't hurt but it seems likely he was overloaded. In any case he came over the Fourways crossroads without stopping but by luck it was clear at the time, then he managed to force the vehicle into a lower gear, heaven knows that could have been a dangerous enough procedure if he had missed it but . . .' There was a longish pause while each of them had a moment's contemplation. '. . . as he came down the main street he was sounding his horn but he couldn't mount the pavement because of pedestrians. But anyway, as he reached the corner he managed to ram one of those concrete lamp standards, you know,' his brief laugh was devoid of amusement, 'those things we always said have spoiled the town. It didn't quite stop him but just at that very moment Simon turned out of the assize courts and was in the wrong spot at the wrong time. The lamp standard fell on to his car and the lorry slewed round and hit him sideways. He was knocked right across the road and through the window of the greengrocer's shop.'

'Oh, God.'

'So you see, Leone, just what a lucky escape he had. As it is he's got off rather lightly. The broken leg is unpleasant and the shoulder and bruised ribs extremely uncomfortable. But it could have been so much worse. The doctors are pleased that he had no head injuries, these are the things they really worry about.'

'Poor Simon. So he wasn't . . . knocked unconscious at all.'

'No, apparently not. The fire brigade had to come and cut him out of the car. I arrived just as he was being lifted into the ambulance. I spoke to one of the firemen and he said he was able to tell them where to cut, let them know when they were getting too close for comfort. Even though he was in considerable pain he was was able to exchange a joke with them. Told them to try to keep him in one piece for he was getting married on Saturday.'

'Oh.' This time the tears would not be controlled and she sobbed for a few minutes before pulling herself together. 'Sorry.' She dabbed at her eyes. 'Maybe we ought to be going along to see if he's awake.'

'Sure you're all right now?'

'I'm fine.' The statement was undermined by her attempt at a smile. 'And I don't want him to wake and find I'm still not there.'

'Oh, don't worry.' He kept his hand under her elbow as they walked back to the private ward. 'That was just Meggy's exaggeration. He didn't really wake. Just moved slightly and murmured something that could have been your name. But now,' as they reached the door he lowered his voice, 'I'm sure it can't be too long before he comes round from the anaesthetic.'

But it was another twenty minutes before Simon moved his head a fraction on the pillow, opened his eyes and looked straight at Leone. His lips moved but she had to lean towards him to catch her own name.

'Simon.' She took his hand and held it to her cheek. 'How are you feeling?'

'Ghastly.' He smiled faintly as the eyelids dropped

over his eyes again. Then, as if she had been waiting
outside the door with the express purpose of repelling
visitors the sister swept into the room, took the
patient's pulse while she looked at them all severely.

'Now,' she adjusted the covers fractionally, 'I think
you should all go and let the patient rest.' There was
the unspoken suggestion that she had arrived just in
time to prevent a riotous drinking party. 'He needs all
the sleep he can get now.'

Obediently they all stood but Leone, conscious as
always of this particular sister's dislike, leaned forward
to kiss Simon's cheek.

'You know,' Mrs Darcy's voice was not entirely
steady, 'you know that my son and Miss Chevenix are
being married on Saturday, Sister.' Her manner would
have melted stones but had little effect on this woman.

'I believe I did hear something about it,' she said in
a voice which implied total lack of interest and which
made Leone fume.

Of course you know about it, the violet eyes
flashed an angry message. You've always been more
than a little interested in Simon yourself. Don't try to
pretend that you hadn't heard quite a lot about
Saturday's arrangements.

But if the message got through there was little
response from Sister Janet Maine, although someone
less upset than Leone might have observed a slight
tightening of the lips. Coolly she allowed her eyes to
travel over Leone's tall elegant figure, their darkness
seeming to pass a comment on the pale yellow trouser-
suit, the expensive handbag and finally on the huge
diamond on her engagement finger.

'Well, I'm sorry but I think you have no choice but
to cancel whatever plans you have for Saturday.' Her
impassive manner did not totally conceal the satisfaction she felt in giving such advice. 'You may see

Doctor Smythe of course but I'm sure he'll merely confirm what I have said.'

And Leone, while disliking the woman, feeling certain that her prognosis was affording her positive pleasure, could not subdue the relief that was sweeping through her in a second shameful tide.

There was little point, Leone assured herself as she drove in through the hospital gates, parking her car with some difficulty in the overcrowded visitors' area, little point in saying anything to Simon till he was well on the way to recovery. He was much better now that almost a week had passed, Saturday had been a difficult day but he had come to terms with the cancelled arrangements and now was sitting up in bed engaging in light-hearted banter with the hospital staff. But he still wasn't ready to cope with the utter shock that her breaking the engagement was bound to bring. It would be time enough when he was properly · convalescent, she assured herself as she walked along the corridor towards his room.

To her surprise there was the sound of voices, of laughter as she placed her fingers on the doorknob and when her light knock wasn't even answered she opened the door and went in.

'Hello, Simon.' As usual she went to the bed, leaning across to kiss his forehead. 'I brought you these.' And she placed the tissue-wrapped bunch of roses on top of the cage which kept the weight of bedclothes from his legs.

'Darling.' He looked much more cheerful than he had done since the accident. 'Isn't this the most wonderful surprise? Guess who's here.'

Leone smiled, looked towards the corner of the room and the tall figure lounging in a chair, the figure of which she had been potently aware since the moment she stepped inside. 'I can't guess,' she heard herself saying gaily. 'But don't keep me in suspense, Simon.'

Just then the figure uncurled himself from the chair and she looked into dark eyes which were faintly yet distinctly mocking, she had a suspicion, vague and unwelcome, hardening as the visitor did a slow survey of her figure. And Simon's introduction immediately confirmed what his excited manner had suggested.

'It's Gray, darling. Gray Ellison.'

'How wonderful.' Trying to inject a note of enthusiasm which would sound genuine to her fiancé, Leone walked round the bed and held out her hand, found herself dwarfed by the tall figure in a way which she didn't quite like. 'I've . . . I've heard such a lot about you.' It was mortifying to hear the note of quivering uncertainty in her voice. She pulled herself together, remembered exactly her reasons for disliking this man and made sure her words were qualified by the chilling expression in her eyes.

'Whereas I,' the narrowing of his eyes as they skimmed her features, the tautness of his smile assured her he had got the message, 'hardly knew of your existence till a moment ago.'

Liar, Leone said silently as she snatched her fingers away, turned from the look in those knowledgeable eyes, eyes which seemed to sum her up in a keen glance and to judge her. Guilty of course. She looked at Simon but he appeared to be oblivious to the appeal in her eyes, for he made only a half-hearted attempt to deny what his friend had said.

'Come on, Gray, if you hadn't gone off on a jaunt round the world you would have known precisely what was happening back here. But now that you've met her, don't you think she's stunning?'

'I'd better not say what I think.' Gray Ellison waited

till Leone had taken the seat beside Simon's bed before resuming his own and allowing a bland smile to encompass them both. 'You, Simon, might not like it.' Nor you, his eyes flicked a message at Leone.

Silently she blazed with anger at him. How dared he avoid answering Simon's very natural question? It wasn't as if he would have found it all that difficult to agree, no great compromise with a strictly honest nature would have been required, always supposing he had such a nature, which she begged leave to doubt.

Impatiently she rose slightly from her chair, flicking the skirts of her pink linen dress beneath her with a practised hand, looking icily at the visitor for a split second before she turned with an especially sweet smile for her fiancé. But he was looking towards his old schoolfriend, for once ignoring the girl he was in love with.

'Of course, I know you, Gray. Can't resist the prettiest girl wherever you are.' And Leone knew that too. Simon had told her too often about his racy friend for her ever to have any misapprehensions about him. 'Usually you get her but this time,' at last his fingers reached out, took the hand Leone had been offering for ages, 'you've come on the scene too late. She's already spoken for. And if it hadn't been for this damned leg, she would be a great deal more than just spoken for by this time.'

Leone felt a slow blush start in the soles of her feet and work its way upwards till her cheeks were burning. It wasn't just that Simon, normally the most prudish of men, should make such a remark, she was filled with a powerful fury at the implication that any advances made by Gray Ellison would have had the least chance of success. In a determination to disabuse him of any such idea she glared across the bed at him, resenting the comfortable way he was sprawled back in his chair, hating the lazy, knowing way he returned her look.

'Then,' his voice was filled with slow amusement and although he was only humouring his friend she knew his words had an especial message for her, 'it's just as well I came back when I did.' And quite deliberately it seemed he guided the conversation away from the personal, excluding her as he and Simon brought themselves up to date on other old friends. And leaving Leone in peace and quiet to make an assessment of the man whose name she had grown heartily sick of in the years since she and Simon had got to know each other properly, whom she had actively disliked in the few months since they had become engaged.

Wonderman, that was her private reference for him, and looking at him now it seemed an accurate enough description. Unarguably good-looking, even if he was a bit larger than life. Now, tall, dark and handsome, that cliché really did apply to Gray Ellison, she decided sarcastically. If you cared for that type. He could have been an ad for someone's expensive after-shave or ski-wear, a flash of those white teeth against the dark skin and all the women would have been rushing for the products which would transform their men into look-alikes.

Obligingly, at that very moment he grinned at something Simon was saying, but glancing in Leone's direction the smile faded just a little and a wary look came into his eyes, almost as if he knew he was being weighed up and found wanting. A novel experience for him, she had no doubt, and her cool look was intended to remind him of just that.

Gray Ellison. Gray Ellison. Gray Ellison. There had been times when she thought she would scream aloud if she heard that name just once more. Gray says this,

Gray says that, every bit of excitement that had ever come into Simon's life had it seemed been by kind permission of Gray Ellison. Since the first day when they had arrived together, new boys at their public school, they had been friends but there had never been the least doubt which was leader. Not Simon, he was too nice to have the qualities of leadership, that is, bossiness, Leone told herself.

'Of course Gray was a scholarship boy,' Simon had droned while telling her of the hilarious day a pair of matron's bloomers had appeared on the flagpole just as a local dignatory was due to come and inspect the school training corps. Simon, of course, had avoided mention of the exact nature of the garment which had replaced the union flag, so assiduously that she was left in little doubt.

'Yes, I know.' Leone had yawned, trying to switch off for a few minutes.

'But none the worse for that of course. His family is poor but they're all frightfully brainy, his mother and father are both Oxford graduates.'

And athletic. And popular. And wonderful. All the other tales about Simon and Gray, rather, she made the mental correction, Gray and Simon had confirmed these facts, his progress through Cambridge had been a similar triumph with Gray Ellison carrying everything before him, taking off every prize in the place and generally being a nauseating pain in the neck. The thought gave her a great deal of quiet satisfaction.

But poor. She returned from her musings to give him a quick glance from behind a sweep of long dark lashes. Poor, Gray Ellison may once have been, it went without saying that he had had to work his way through university, but poor he certainly did not look now. Her eyes dropped to her fingers linked with Simon's, then she leaned forward a little to confirm the impression of shoes in finest calf, one foot swaying gently, suede trousers flaring slightly, long, dark fingers linked and showing what she was sure was a pure silk cuff and a very expensive looking gold watch.

Too late she was aware of dark eyes surveying her sardonically, obviously amused by such blatant interest, but she refused to be embarrassed this time and stared back coldly. And took in each detail of the fine tweed jacket, the fawn tie with swirls of muted orange, hair dark, longish, falling in a deep wave over one temple.

'. . . Isn't it, Leone?' Only then, realising that Simon, in fact both men, were waiting for her to comment on some point, did she feel another blush sweep across her cheek. And she had to wrench her attention away, back to Simon.

'I'm sorry . . . I'm afraid I've been dreaming. You see, you were talking about your friends, people I don't know.'

'Oh, darling, I'm sorry.' His manner was so apologetic that she couldn't avoid glancing at Gray Ellison to see if he had noticed. He had. Of course. And the darkly amused eyes, raised eyebrows were telling her just that. 'I simply got carried away. And I'm afraid I was running on a bit. You know what I'm like, darling.' He squeezed her hand, smiled fatuously.

'You were saying.' She extricated her fingers, reached out for the flowers which she suddenly decided must be dying of thirst. 'What were you saying, Simon?' She walked to the wash basin in the corner of the room, turned to smile at him.

'I was saying, isn't it wonderful to think that Gray has sailed all the way from Cape Town in his yacht?'

'Wonderful.' Her voice was neutral but she was in such a position that her glance towards the visitor conveyed a hint of sarcasm. 'We're hearing so much about the daring of lone yachtsmen these days that . . .'

'Oh, don't credit me with too much daring.' The deep voice was humorous but with just enough edge to be a warning. 'I've never claimed to be a lone yachtsman.' His smile sparkled with animosity.

'Oh,' sharply she turned from him, adjusting her smile for Simon's benefit, 'then I've misunderstood. But as I said, I wasn't listening properly.'

'I'm sure you must have found our conversation boring,' he said tightly as he rose to his feet. 'I think I'd better be off then, Simon.'

'Oh, must you?' He did not trouble to hide the disappointment he felt at the prospect of being left alone with his fiancée and Leone transferred her reproving glance to him. But before any more could be said the door opened and Sister Maine came into the room.

'Visitors still here?' It wasn't really a question, more a request that they should be on their way. 'Everyone from the main ward has been gone for ages.'

'I brought these for Mr Darcy.' Leone indicated the roses which she had left in the basin. 'There doesn't seem to be a vase.'

'I'll have one of the nurses see to that.' Sister Maine was in charge here and wanted everyone to know she didn't concern herself with the menial chores. Calmly she returned Leone's stormy look before sliding an interested glance in the direction of the second, infinitely more intriguing visitor. 'Then I'll give you just half a minute more, Simon.' She smiled almost skittishly towards the patient and left the room.

'That woman,' Leone began through clenched teeth but it seemed she was the only person annoyed by the effrontery of the nurse, Simon at least was too excited to hear any adverse comments his fiancée might be making about Janet Maine.

'I've just had a great idea.' His face shone with the pleasure his thoughts were affording. 'Look, darling, Gray doesn't have a car so why don't you run him back to the harbour? And, Gray,' before Leone could think of an excuse to refuse he had transferred his attention to his friend, 'you have nothing to do tonight, why don't you take Leone out for the evening? She's at a loose end and so are you. It would mean a lot to me if you would cheer her up while I'm in hospital.'

CHAPTER TWO

THEY had reached the car before either of them spoke,
Leone trusting the angry tapping of her heels on the
polished floors of the hospital to convey her thoughts.
But as she unlocked the passenger door for him,
leaning across to undo the catch with an ungraciously
petulant gesture, she broke the silence.

'There's no need you know.' The key was turned in
the ignition, the engine revved impatiently as he slid
into the confined space beside her, snapping the seat
belt confidently.

'No need?' he enquired with irritating calm,
studying her as she gave all her attention to
negotiating the car out of its confined space.

'No need to feel obliged to take me out tonight.'

'Of course there's no need but I'd like to.'

'Honestly?' It was thrown sarcastically in his
direction as she steered skilfully out into the lane of
traffic.

'Honestly,' he concurred. 'You mustn't be too
modest, Miss Chevenix.'

'I wasn't being.' Trust him to take things up the
wrong way. Or at least to *pretend* to misunderstand,
for she had no doubt he was aware of the exact
meaning of her words.

'So,' she spared the briefest of glances in his
direction, 'you really want to take me out this
evening.'

'Believe me, if I didn't, the fact that you and Simon
are engaged wouldn't have persuaded me.'

Her snort was supposed to indicate total scepticism

but he didn't rise to it and when he showed no inclination to engage in polite chit-chat she considered letting the matter drop. But then, 'I resent Simon palming me off on his friends.'

'I told you . . .'

Now that she was alone with him it was more difficult to ignore his voice. Already she had been made aware of its deep timbre but now she detected the slightest of accents, something superimposed on the standard English public school voice, probably due to the years he had spent in the States and apparently in South Africa. It added something intensely masculine, so macho a trickle of irritation ran down her spine. She tried to concentrate on what he was saying.

'. . . there was no palming off,' the pause was slightly prolonged, 'unless what you really mean is that you hate the idea of Simon imposing his old acquaintances on you.'

'That wasn't what I was thinking of,' she said tartly, but his question did force her to acknowledge the idea that had been floating somewhere at the back of her mind.

'Good,' he said crisply as they reached the harbour area of the town. 'And I promise not to bore you too much with tales of my misspent youth. Along there.' He directed with an imperious wave of one hand towards the jetty. 'Second boat from the end.'

Leone pulled up with a savage little jerk, meant to indicate that she was not to be regarded as a taxi driver. She engaged reverse gear even while he was extricating his long legs from the recesses of the car, waited with what she hoped was obvious impatience.

'This is it.' If he had noticed her hint then he had decided for the sake of irritation to keep her hanging about, the door held wide open so she could obtain the best possible view of his wonderful yacht.

And the *Sea Trekker*, its name immaculately inscribed on the glistening hull, was worth looking at. Although she knew next to nothing about boats even Leone could recognise that and if she hadn't then the small admiring group of small boys and middle-aged men would have told her so. In the warm summer sunshine the varnished superstructure gleamed and every visible piece of brass appeared to have been polished all the way from Cape Town.

The group of spectators moved and divided, enabling Leone to see what had previously been hidden from her. On the prow of the ship a girl was leaning over the rail, the breeze was tossing an already disarranged mane of blonde hair. She was wearing tight white jeans, rolled up to show slender ankles and calves, tanned to a deep honey shade; on top, a broadly striped blue and white T-shirt only just managed to contain the generous curves bestowed by nature. Which might have been the reason for at least some of the fascinated interest shown by the gawping males.

'Would you care to come and look over her now?'

'What?' Leone surveyed the face which suddenly intruded between her and the girl, her skin colouring as she imagined for a wild instant that he had been able to see into her mind.

'The boat I mean.' He spoke so drily that he might just as well have said, 'not the girl'. 'Would you like to come and look over the *Trekker*?'

'No, oh no thank you.' She tried to engage reverse gear again but stopped when she heard the awful grating sound. And she took her foot from the accelerator. 'Look I must go.' But his head was still inside the car.

'When shall I pick you up?'

'Oh, have you a car? I thought . . .'

'By this evening I shall have a car. I don't like being driven round by my dates.'

'Well, I'm not that.' Her smile was chilly.

'We have a date for this evening I take it.'

'If you insist.'

'I insist. I'll pick you up at seven-thirty.'

'Quarter to eight would be better.' She said out of perversity.

'Seven-thirty.' He repeated as if she had not spoken. 'I'm looking forward to it. You intrigue me, Miss Chevenix.' And before she could say a word, let alone think of some crushing reply, he had slammed the door decisively. She let the engine roar but saw from the corner of her eye that he had turned away without troubling to wait. His feet were ascending the gangway as she moved off with an angry little jerk and she was unable to see what happened when he met the girl.

She was still angry when she stood in front of the mirror putting the last touches to her make-up before going downstairs. For two pins and if she had any way of getting into contact with him she would have called the whole thing off. She didn't want to spend a whole evening in the company of Gray Ellison and she saw no reason why she should. Not even to please Simon. Surely, *surely*, she applied the last little flick of mascara to her lashes, it ought to please Simon more that she didn't want to go out with his best friend.

Come to that, she sank down on to the stool and surveyed herself with eyes limpidly dark and despairing, surely knowing what he did about his friend, Simon ought not to be risking his fiancée to this extent? The implication in everything she had been told about him was that Gray Ellison was irresistible to women, that most women threw themselves at him and that Gray, being the man he was, accepted what was so blatantly offered.

That was probably why he had this condescending view of marriage, that it was all right for women and fools but best avoided by any man who had the faintest shred of self-respect. Of course a man like him didn't have to bother about the ties implied by any lasting relationship, not when he could have his choice of all the women who swam into his orbit.

But not me. Leone picked up a lipstick and smeared it over her lips. Definitely not me. He had been irritating her for years with his reported remarks and especially since she had become engaged to Simon. That remark about not knowing of her existence. When he had had the cheek to send Simon a cable with the single word —'*Don't*'—written on it. That had made her so angry she was unable to recognise the inconsistency of her own reactions. All these weeks trying to think of a reason for extricating herself from the situation and yet resenting . . .

Oh, with an angry whirl she rose from her seat, turning from her reflection with a speed which sent her filmy skirts swaying about her slim legs in a shimmer of deep blues and greens, she must have been mad to agree with it.

'I really think it's rather strange of Simon,' Lady Chevenix complained, '*asking* someone to take you out for him.'

'I don't see why.' Sir Piers rose from the chair he habitually occupied, went to the sideboard where he began to fiddle about with glasses and decanters, 'Sherry, Enid? Leone?' Are you sure you won't?' Over his shoulder he glanced towards where his daughter was sitting, waiting.

'Quite sure, Father.' Difficult to explain that she felt

it best to keep her wits about her when she was going
out with this dangerous man.

'No, I don't see why.' After handing a sherry to his
wife, Sir Piers took up the conversation again as he
sipped from his own glass. 'It seems eminently
sensible of Simon, he's probably beginning to realise
just how much of a strain the last week has been for
Leone.'

'Not *just* on her.' Lady Chevenix spoke with
suffering.

'No, not just on her. You, my dear, have been
marvellous.' As he flattered his wife Sir Piers dropped
the faintest of winks in his daughter's direction. They
both understood how Lady Chevenix thought she was
the most put-upon and harassed of women, in spite of
having an extremely efficient staff and a daughter who
took on all the jobs the mother disliked. 'As you
always are.'

'But still,' she was marginally cheered and just a
little bit flirtatious, 'I can't imagine you in similar
circumstances insisting that I go out with one of your
friends. Not if you were lying injured in hospital.'

'Ah, but then, I had a jealous and suspicious nature.
Especially as far as you were concerned. Clearly
Simon is altogether more trusting.' He looked at his
wife without the vestige of a smile.

'Yes, well, isn't that what I'm saying? Maybe Simon
ought to be suspicious of this . . . Gray something or
other. I do know something about him you know. I
know he came to stay with Meggy and John when the
boys were at university together and she didn't care
for him much at all. She thought he had much too
much influence over Simon, not always for the good I
might add.'

'But then,' Sir Piers paused to light a cigar, puffed
away for a few minutes till it was well alight, 'Meggy

would resent anyone who threatened her own influence over the boy. She has always been inclined to treat him as her pet lamb, in fact it was a surprise to me that she allowed him to go away to school at all.'

'Of course he had to go to school, his father had been to Pendlebury,' Lady Chevenix said as if that was an irrefutable argument. 'Besides, I won't have you talking like that about Meggy. I've known her since I was a girl,' she went on with the same logic.

'I know, I know.' Sir Piers sighed in good-humoured capitulation. 'All I am saying, my dear, is that none of us is perfect and that includes Meggy Darcy.'

Leone sat without taking much part in the conversation but it was surprising how what she had heard seemed to be underlining her own dissatisfaction with her engagement. For Simon *was* a mother's boy. Just a little bit, and it was his mother's fault more than his. But still, what man in his mid-thirties had to ring her up to report, to ask her permission almost, when he thought he might be an hour late in reaching home. It wasn't, Leone had told herself mutinously more than once, as if he was suggesting he stay out all night. Not that such a blindly passionate idea would ever have occurred to him.

'I think, my dear, that's your young man arriving.'

'Oh is it? Then maybe I should just . . .' In a kind of reflex panic action her hand went out to snatch up her bag and she got to her feet.

'No.' Her mother insisted calmly. 'Just sit down till he's shown in, Leone. I want to know just who it is you are going out with.' And Leone sat down on her chair with just as much submission as Simon would ever have shown. She was trying to cope with a sudden agitation in her breathing and a wild tattoo in her pulses. Nothing she couldn't deal with of course.

But, to her surprise, the interval with her parents seemed to go pretty agreeably. But it would have been strange if it hadn't considering just how smooth Gray Ellison could be when he exerted himself. To begin with he was immaculately dressed in the conservative manner most likely to appeal to Lady Chevenix—dark suit, white shirt with the narrowest of pink stripes and dark red tie, all worn with the casual dash which only the most distinguished of men could muster.

He could hardly have looked more handsome, Leone thought sourly as she completed the introductions; she sensed that her mother was actually disappointed when, with a guilty little shrug of the shoulders and an apologetic grin he refused the offer of a drink.

'Some other time, if you're kind enough to ask me,' he glanced at his wrist watch, 'the restaurant where we've booked only managed to squeeze us in at the last minute and they were fairly insistent that we should show up by eight. I would hate to disappoint your daughter,' although he didn't even look at Leone as he spoke with obvious sincerity to her mother, there was something about his manner which aroused suspicion, 'and Simon of course by not providing her with dinner as I promised.'

'Well,' Lady Chevenix fluttered, quite forgetting how averse she had been to seeing her daughter going out with this man, 'if you do get stuck then come back here. We don't eat till eight-thirty and there is always enough. . .'

'I'm sure it will be all right, Mother,' Leone interrupted. 'Besides, I don't know any restaurants who are quite as strict clock-watchers.' I'm sure we'll get something to eat. Shall we go?' She asked her escort in a way that suggested it was a boring affair she'd rather have over and done with, and led the way out to the car.

They drove some way in silence, Leone affecting intense interest in the lush foliage of the summer verges as the town was left behind and they took the coast road, but at last he spoke.

'Am I allowed to say how very pretty you look?'

'If you mean it then of course you're allowed.' She could hardly have explained why she persisted in such a sarcastic manner of speaking except that she was with Gray Ellison and that itself was explanation enough. But she was surprised by the suffusion of pleasure that caught her unawares, thrilling her in a way that Simon's compliments never did.

'Only very rarely do I say things I don't mean.'

'Really?' In spite of her determination to pay him as little attention as possible she turned round in her seat so she could see the strong, slightly aquiline dark profile. 'So ... you're different from most people then?'

'Different from you, do you mean? Are you always saying things you don't mean? I must remember.'

The comment deserving only to be treated with contempt, she didn't trouble to answer and sat round in her seat again. But he wouldn't let her escape.

'A compliment should be accepted graciously.'

'Even when it's insincere.'

'Especially then I should have thought. Anyway,' she sensed a slanting glance in her direction, 'I wasn't being insincere as you must know. You don't strike me as a naïve little thing who doesn't know her own worth. Besides,' now he was faintly scoffing, 'you must have spent hours in front of the mirror achieving that effect.'

'To come out with you?'

'Why not?' Now he was quite openly laughing at

her. 'I went to some trouble to get ready for you. I was hoping you'd have noticed.'

It was difficult to stop her lips curving in response but she did. 'Really?' She spoke with assumed indifference but hadn't quite the courage to say she hadn't noticed. Not when every inch of her was powerfully aware of the man sitting by her side.

'I did.' He had swung into the car park of an hotel and pulled on the brake with such savagery that she could hear the wheels skidding briefly on the gravel. 'I did.' He repeated between clenched teeth as he pulled her round to face him. 'And you'd better damn well know it.'

Leone's eyes widened in unexpected alarm at the expression she saw on his face. It wasn't so much anger or irritation, those she could have recognised as the emotions she had so single-mindedly set out to arouse, but there was more to it than that. His eyes, of a deep, dark brown, amber-flecked now that she was close enough to study them, seemed to hint at unaccountably fiery passions and now were fixed on her mouth in a manner that was quite unmistakable. Nervously, she passed her tongue over her lips, unable to wrench her eyes away from his, a shudder rippled through her as the fingers tightened on her shoulders, gave her a tiny shake as if attempting to force some sense into her. 'Let's go,' he growled.

When she got out of the car Leone held on to the door for a moment till the shakiness had gone from her knees. Several people were walking slowly towards the hotel and two of them were giving her curious glances. Damn, she thought, as she recognised a couple who were clients of Simon, what on earth would they be thinking seeing her out with a stranger so soon after the postponed wedding? The brilliant smile she gave them suggested they had no need for concern, the brief nod she received in reply indicated they were reserving their judgement. And the possessive way Gray Ellison kept his hand on her elbow, something she was grateful for in view of her four inch heels and the roughness of the ground, would have done nothing to lull their suspicions. Leone was positively relieved when they were settled at a table close to a window where they had an unrestricted view of a rugged length of coast and with several unoccupied tables round about.

'The others,' she buried her head in the long and tempting menu, 'don't appear to have been so intimidated by the time proviso.'

'What?' He looked up and round and grinned. 'No, they don't do they?'

And Leone, apparently intent on the menu again, was aware of her heart hammering against her chest in a way that was both uncomfortable and inexplicable.

'It was very clever of you . . .' The waiter had taken the orders and had provided them with drinks. '. . . to find this place. It has only just reopened after a change of hands.'

'I made some enquiries, this place was re-commended. If the meal is as good as the situation then we shan't complain.' He paused, looking down at his glass while she, fascinated by the long dark fingers playing with the stem, did the same.

'I . . . I think it should be.' There was definitely something wrong with her behaving so idiotically, hardly able to carry on a conventional conversation. 'I've . . . heard good reports.'

'You've never been here with Simon then?' Now he was lying back in his chair, surveying her through those disturbing eyes. 'I should have thought this was the very place an up-and-coming young solicitor would have brought his . . .' he paused and his eyes once again appeared to focus on her mouth, '. . . fiancée.'

'Simon,' this time her supreme effort was rewarded for she spoke without a tremor, 'is hardly that. He's a senior partner in the oldest law firm in the area. His great-grandfather started the practice in eighteen . . .'

'Oh, forgive me,' he begged mendaciously. 'Of course I ought to have remembered that he has arrived. I quite forgot about the past generations of Darcys.' He spoke the name as if it deserved only amusement.

'Well really . . .' It was a gasp of sheer indignation, but before she could expand the waiter, and he too had a very familiar look, came up with the first courses which he placed in front of them. Leone found herself grinding pepper on to her baked avocado with a liberality she was to regret for the rest of the meal but said nothing while the waiter fiddled with a bottle of wine.

'You really are . . .' she hissed across the table the moment she was free to do so, '. . . the absolute end.'

'I should go easy on the pepper,' he said calmly. 'Unless you have an absolute passion for the stuff that is.'

'Here you are.' She thrust the offending object towards him.

'Mmm,' he considered his dish, 'I know some people do but I don't think I will. Not when the melon is drenched in port.' And he seemed not to notice the poisonous look she gave him.

For the rest of the meal Leone wondered if she alone was feeling the strain. Certainly he showed few signs, but chatted amiably and entertainingly enough of the journey he had just completed, only nothing he could say could possibly, so Leone assured herself as she stabbed viciously at an inoffensive piece of meringue, placate her. How dared he patronise Simon, especially when Simon idolised him so much.

'Shall we go?' He interrupted her brooding thoughts and at once, deliberately showing him how anxious she was for the evening to end, Leone got to her feet. But when they were back in the car she found to her annoyance that instead of heading back in the direction they had come, he turned right coming out of the gate and drove further along the coast road.

'Do you mind! I would prefer to go straight back to town.'

'Just bear with me. There's a little cove where Simon brought me once, years ago. I'm curious to know if it's still unspoiled. Or have they built a ten storey hotel, complete with funfair?'

'I should think it highly unlikely. Planning regulations are fairly strict in this part of the country.'

'Oh, I'm sure.'

'You sound as if you disapprove,' she flared, turning round so she had a clear view of his profile in pale moonlight. 'If you enjoy seeing landscapes ruined I could recommend some stretches of the Costa Brava or the Riviera.'

'Or come to that, some parts of London. For a view to make conservationists foam at the mouth, that ruined skyline takes some beating.'

'We . . .' Rather dismayed by having the wind so completely taken from her sails she floundered for something to say. 'I didn't know we were talking about London,' she finished lamely.

'Neither were we.' As he spoke, tersely through closed lips, he swung off the road, taking a narrow track which she would never have dared negotiate with her small car, the bushes seeming to crowd in on them until quite suddenly they were actually in a tiny private cove with a pebble beach and waves lapping over it in a crescent.

'I thought this must be it.' He spoke with a shade of self-satisfaction. 'I suppose you and Simon come here from time to time.'

It would be too humiliating to admit that she had never seen the spot before so she took refuge in a lie. 'Not often.'

He switched off the engine and dropped the keys in his pocket. 'You sound annoyed. Have I intruded into one of your sentimental meeting spots?'

'Don't be silly.' She longed to tell him to start the car and drive her home but she had a feeling he would take delight in deciding to thwart her so she sat quite still, her fingers clutching the strap of her handbag as if it were in danger of being snatched. But she gasped as she felt him turn towards her, drew in a nervous breath as his fingers caught at her shoulders pulling her round to face him.

'What is the matter with you, for heaven's sake? What's so silly about a man bringing the girl he's in love with along to this quiet spot.' He gave every indication of being amused rather than irritated by her attitude. 'It seems to me a perfectly natural reaction.'

'You would think so. But Simon isn't the least bit like you.'

There was a long silence during which they looked at each other. Leone wondered if he could hear the thump of her heart against her ribs, the sound seemed to fill the entire vehicle.

'Is that why you dislike me so much? Because I'm not Simon?'

'What makes you think I don't like you?' In view of her attitude to him since the instant they had met the question was farcical but she didn't think of that till later. Just then she was too preoccupied with her own angry reaction to his shout of amusement.

'Isn't that the message you've been trying to give me?,

'Do you find it so difficult to accept that someone doesn't like you? It happens in life you know.'

'I know, Leone.' His voice softened and it seemed to her that he had drawn imperceptibly closer, she could feel the warmth of his breath on her cheek and the fingers still resting on her shoulders were suddenly gentle. In the entire evening it was the first time he had used her Christian name and spoken in that peculiarly throbbing way, it was causing havoc. 'I know it happens and it's something we all have to accept but it's you I'm curious about. You admit then that you do dislike me.'

'I neither like nor dislike you.'

'Oh, come on.' His finger traced a brief path down her neck, over before she could protest or resist his unwelcome familiarity. 'Did it happen before we met? Or in that instant when you turned and saw me there in the hospital? Interrupting your idyll with Simon.'

'No, not then.' She strove for calm. 'I suppose maybe I got tired of hearing from Simon how wonderful you always were. Quite frankly, I grew bored by the sound of your name. You were always such a great success.' She closed her lips before she could say any more that she might have cause to regret. It was easy enough to visualise his amusement if she as much as hinted her resentment at his views on marriage. Simon had tried her patience by expressing them at every opportunity and she was not in the mood to listen to a dissertation on the joys of single life from an expert. Well ... single was the wrong word for obviously his attitude was to enjoy all the pleasures but to shoulder none of the responsibilities.

He withdrew from her and without asking her permission took out a cigar, lit it, puffing out smoke through his side window which he wound down.

'And you resent that, of course.' All the throbbing sensuality had gone from his voice, now it was harsh and abrasive which was just as well for it had been making her feel much too emotional. As it was she had difficulty in thinking just exactly what he was talking about. 'Success is not important to Miss Chevenix, daughter of Sir Piers Chevenix, late of the diplomatic corps, born with a silver soup spoon in her mouth, indulged in every way since the moment she drew breath.'

'Why you . . .' What a good thing his manner had cured her of that invading weakness which had been a problem till a moment ago, she was glad that now all her energy could be given to throwing his accusations back at him. And even the fact that they might have contained some truth gave him no right.

'No *you*,' he said bitterly before she had time to gather her thoughts. 'What was it all about, Leone? What tawdry little ideas did you harbour about me in that pathetic little mind of yours? Were you perhaps a little bit jealous on Simon's behalf? Perhaps he didn't quite measure up to the mark you had set for yourself.'

'Jealous?' That word burned in her mind and she threw it back shrilly. 'Why on earth should I be jealous?'

'You tell me.' The sudden quietness of his manner cut across her indignation. 'You tell me, sweetie. But something's burning inside that pretty little breast of yours. And until you recognise it for what it is and go ahead and deal with it, you're going to be pretty miserable and what's worse, you're going to make everyone round you miserable, too. That includes Simon.' He ground out his cigar in the small ashtray with an aggressive gesture and then pushed it closed.

The atmosphere in the car seemed alive with

tension, Leone felt her pulses begin to take off again and in spite of all her efforts she sensed she would be unable to control them. His face was so close to hers, eyes in the darkness still able to express contempt though why should he ... Oh, it was so unfair when ...

'I ... I am perfectly happy about my life thank you, and your diagnosis is miles out. As far as Simon is concerned you're totally wrong. I think we're perfectly suited.' Except that I don't love him and have no intention of marrying him, she reminded herself silently with crossed fingers. 'But maybe you think I should be wildly happy.' Her voice rose as self-pity stuggled with mild hysteria, threatening to bring tears streaming down her cheeks. 'It may ... have escaped your notice but Simon and I should have been married last Saturday. Right now we should have been on the Greek Islands and I have other things on my mind rather than trying to analyse my feelings for you.'

The moment the words were out she wished she could have chosen them with more care, she sat staring at him, her heart thumping against her chest and willing him to ignore the opportunity she had given him. But of course that was the last thing she could expect in her dealings with Gray Ellison.

But even so, he took his time before replying and those seconds were fraught with emotions Leone could hardly begin to understand. 'Sexual frustration, is that what you're saying?' Again he leaned towards her, a hand came out to touch, to caress her skin.

'How like you.' Drawling contempt was her sole defence against the immediate weakness engendered by his touch. 'It's the only kind of thing people like you can think of.'

'And you, Leone,' he insisted, 'are you going to tell me you aren't suffering from that? Because if I were in

Simon's place and thought you weren't, then I'd be a very worried man indeed.'

'But isn't that what I've just been telling you?' She seized the opportunity she had been given. 'You and Simon are very different people.'

'Let's talk about you, shall we? Simon is probably in too much discomfort at the moment to be thinking clearly. Besides, I'm pretty sure that he's in love with you. Whereas you . . .' he paused meaningfully, 'I'm not at all sure why you can be thinking of marrying him.'

'It's a little more than that.' For the time being she had forgotten her own panic at the prospect of the wedding. 'If it hadn't been for the accident he and I would have been married by now. Not just thinking about it.'

'But why, that's what I'm asking, Leone. Why were you going to marry Simon when it's patently obvious that you don't love him?'

'You have no idea whether I love him or not but as it happens, and just to satisfy your morbid curiosity, I do. Otherwise, as you so very cleverly observe, there would be no point, would there?'

'And yet, you deny that you're suffering any sense of frustration.' His fingers trickled down her neck, resting just above her collar bone. 'To me, that seems highly unnatural.'

'Oh . . . people like you. You think sex is the answer to everything. Can't you imagine a love where that isn't the beginning and end of it all?'

'Of course I can imagine it. Just about.' In the dark she saw the swift mocking flash of teeth. 'But I find it hard to imagine in a young couple about to be married. Sex, in the early days at least, is the most potent force in any relationship between a man and a woman. Without it, all the other things pale into insignificance.'

'I'll take your word for that,' Leone said coldly, 'I'm sure you're an expert in that as in most other fields.'

'At least I know it exists. You're a beautiful woman, Leone.' The words brought a rush of emotions into her consciousness, her heart bounding in such agitation that rationality began to desert her. 'And you should know about these things. Your skin should throb when Simon touches you.' One finger stroked the delicate tissue of her neck. 'Your pulses should leap when he's close.' His other hand came out to skim the curve of her breast. 'When he comes to kiss you, your lips should part in welcome.' His voice deepened, grew more disturbing still. 'As they're doing now.'

Truly she had not expected him to kiss her. She was—she struggled with the need to resist him—wholly unprepared for it and perhaps this was why she failed so signally.

To begin with, she had never known that it could be like this. That such a common, unexceptional contact between a man and woman could produce this weakness, this delicious yielding weakness, which once begun induced an inexplicable longing to continue, to give more ... Thoughts evaporated in the wildness of the sensation, his hands moving over the softness of her body, a familiarity which would have been rejected in anyone else, brought her reactions up to boiling point.

'Damn this.' She heard his husky mutter, shivered for a second when she found herself abandoned. Then she was wrenched from the car, there was a note of confidence in the brief laugh as he gathered her into his arms. 'I've never been one for making love in the back of a car.' And his fingers slid down her spine, moulding her suppliant body close to him.

Intoxication. Madness. Fever. Those were just a

few of the words she used afterwards in an attempt to describe and excuse her wholly irrational behaviour. But at the time, when his lips were teasing into life feelings she had not known existed, the only word that came to her was magic.

Magic that might have taken her heaven knows where if something hadn't brought her to her senses in time. But by then they were lying on a knoll of soft grass, he was leaning over her and her fingers were twined in the disordered silkiness of his hair, pressing his lips still closer to the exposed column of her throat. Dreamily she opened her eyes, looked up into the slip of moon now clearly visible in the darkness of the sky. And he had such a cynical, seen-it-all before expression on his face that she was jolted from her sensual wonderland, returned with a thump to the rather sordid situation of being made love to in what was hardly more than a field. And by a man whom she neither knew nor liked.

The determination and calmness with which she suddenly thrust him away were afterwards to give her great satisfaction and pride. At the actual moment they held nothing but anguish. But she stared up into his dark features with as much calmness as it was possible for her to assume.

'Leone.' He said softly, almost caressingly and rolled away from her without another word. When he got to his feet she took the hand he offered and was pulled up but then she spent a few minutes apparently absorbed in brushing some grasses from her dress. But not too absorbed to see that he was straightening his tie, pushing the disordered hair back from his forehead.

Still without speaking, she returned to her seat in the car but her heart was thumping loudly while he reversed the vehicle, skilfully, she was not too agitated to admit, on to the main road. By the time they had driven a few miles she had allowed her own humiliation to be transmuted into indignation with him. No doubt he had dreamed up the ploy about the tiny cove simply to set the scene for a bit of passionate necking. He must have thought it a bit of a joke, trying to break through the barrier she had erected between them. The very idea was enough to inflame her anger against him while at the same time calming her down. If he could behave deviously, set out to conduct an experiment, then two could play the game. With considerable sweetness she turned to the impassive profile.

'I think maybe there was something in what you said.'

'Oh?' Driving as if the devil himself was after them he spared her not a single glance.

'Yes. Your ... theory. I think maybe you were right. Perhaps I am suffering from some kind of frustration.' The stupid admission brought a quick scald of colour to her cheeks and she was grateful for the darkness which hid it. 'As you say, natural enough when you think of the circumstances.'

'Entirely,' he said savagely as he rammed the gear lever forward. 'But I think Simon is going to have one hell of a job to effect a proper cure.'

Leone was so angry with the implications of that she couldn't find her voice for a moment. When she could, she forced herself to go on in the voice that excluded reason.

'I shouldn't let that worry you. Anyway, I'm grateful for your help, the little experiment seems to have worked. I'm feeling much less tense now.'

'Good,' he said sarcastically as he turned into the wide gates of her home. 'It should save you a pound or two for psychiatric advice.'

Leone clenched her teeth to stop the quick retort which would have let him see how much his words had angered her. 'I don't think I was in *that* much of a state.' As he drew to a halt in front of the front door, she paused with her hand on the door handle. 'But as I said, it has been a valuable experience.' Her laugh was light and she hoped, condescending.

'Very, I should say.'

'Well,' her nerves were pretty close to breaking point, 'at least it proved one thing, that you would *not* make a satisfactory substitute for Simon. So I'll just have to put up with my ... sexual frustration you called it I think, till I can get Simon to the altar.'

'Really,' he leaned across her so purposefully that she recoiled in alarm, felt furious when he laughed softly as if he knew what she expected, 'if you think that's going to cure you ... think again.'

Furiously she got out of the car and slammed the door but found her entrance to her home blocked by his powerful figure.

'Good night.' He took her fingers to his lips and kissed them, she suspected he was only too well aware of the throb that ran through her body. 'If things become too difficult, just get in touch. I don't mind a bit being used as a therapist.'

And a moment later she was watching the lights of his car disappearing into the night.

CHAPTER THREE

THE house was silent, faint moonlight slanted mysteriously through the tall window as she crossed the hall and ran soundlessly upstairs to her bedroom. Reaching it, she leaned against the door as if she had found sanctuary after a long and hazardous chase.

But gradually her racing pulses subsided, she heaved a deep shuddering sigh and levered herself, acutely conscious of overwhelming emotional exhaustion, away from the door. She walked over to the dressing-table and slumped on to the stool.

It was true what he had said, her mind in spite of her agitation was clear and every word they had exchanged was firmly recorded. She picked out the ones that applied at this particular moment. 'You have spent hours in front of the mirror achieving that effect.' He had said that and it would be useless to deny it to herself as she had tried to do with him. Dispassionately she leaned forward, closely examining the face that was so familiar to her. It was equally futile to deny that the results of those hours of preparation had long since gone, swept away in those fevered minutes of passion on the beach in the cove.

But there was another change in her. The blue eyes, always intense and brilliant, had taken on a more vulnerable aspect, the bruised lips parted, quivering a little as certain thoughts, forceful and bewildering emotions returned to disturb her. There was this dress, a faltering hand touched the narrow shoulder straps beneath the filmy bolero, why on earth had she chosen to wear one of her favourite honeymoon dresses for an outing she didn't want with a man she didn't like?

There, her wide mouth curved in self-contempt, there was a question for the psychiatrist if you like. Then, without thinking what she was doing, she seized a swathe of the night-dark hair which fell to her shoulders, twisting it into a dishevelled bundle on top of her head. She might just decide the time had come for a new hair style. She leaned forward, giving her reflection a sultry provocative look that for no reason at all increased her heart beat.

A picture flashed into her mind, a curvaceous girl, her hair bleached and disordered by sun and wind, her smile showing white teeth, almost as if she were waiting to have her picture taken. It was just a split second before Leone's shocked mind recognised the blonde who had lounged against the rail of the yacht, another stunning instant while she absorbed her own reflection, a conscious imitation of that unknown sexy female.

With a gesture of disgust she got up from her seat, whirling away from the mirror, hands pressed against her ears as if she would block out mocking male laughter. And it was only after she had stepped out of a long and cool shower that she felt some of her shaming feelings had been washed away, that she was able to smile, however wanly, at the wholly ridiculous concept that she was jealous of Gray Ellison's travelling companion, that she was in any way seeing her as a rival. She didn't even *like* the man, after all.

A week later and she had returned to blissful normality. Thanks largely to the fact that she hadn't in the meantime set eyes on the source of her restlessness. She hadn't quite tossed him out of her mind but she was working on it. It wasn't made any easier by Simon's apparent determination to bring up the subject of Gray Ellison at every opportunity.

'Can you reach up for that box of buttered brazils, Leone?' She was busy pouring some tea in the hospital shop when her colleague made the request, bringing her mind back from the subject which was half-way to an obsession, in spite of all her determination to make it otherwise.

'Yes, if you'll take these cups I'll get them for you.' Leone was used to such requests, her height being an advantage for the upper shelves. But when she turned round with the box in her hand, annoyance drove the colour from her face as she looked into the dark assessing eyes of the man who was never far from her thoughts. Then, almost as if turned by a tap the blood came blazing back into her cheeks, no doubt offering little Miss Barnett who was dividing her time equally between them, much room for interesting speculation.

'Oh.' The heat was slowly subsiding and she forced her lips into what could be mistaken for a smile. 'Hello. You wanted these?'

'Yes.' There was a faint frown on his face. 'I thought I'd take them to Simon. They always were a favourite of his as you know.'

'Oh, oh yes.' The very fact that she had known no such thing made it all the more important to agree. Then, almost at once suspecting a trap she looked at him suspiciously. 'That will be one seventy-five, please.' She took the note and fiddled a moment or two with the change. 'I'm afraid,' her eyes sparkled as she turned again to face him, pulled back her hand as he appeared to linger too long in accepting the notes and coins she held out to him, 'I'm afraid you won't get in if that's where you're going now. Sister Maine is on duty and she is a martinet.'

'Oh, Sister and I have an understanding.' He

grinned and leaned an elbow on the formica counter, giving her an opportunity to have a closer look at bare forearms, tanned to a shade just a bit lighter than mahogany, and an expanse of bare chest, sprinkled with dark curling hair, that was just short of indecent at this time of the morning. She forced herself to pay no attention . . . he and that show-off girl on the boat were a pair . . .

'Of course,' she said with the cool sarcasm which they both understood, then noticing the glance of sparkling amusement he slid in the direction of Miss Barnett she began some introductions. 'Mr Ellison is an old friend of Simon's.' It seemed appropriate to disarm any suspicions the older woman might have.

'I thought you might be frantically busy.' Gray looked round the almost empty waiting room then back at Miss Barnett who simpered under his attractive smile.

'No, this morning we have fewer clinics than usual. One of our surgeons is on holiday and that makes a difference to the outpatients. And how is dear Simon?' She looked up at him besottedly.

'Oh, I think he's making progress. At least, according to Sister Maine.' The glance he flicked at Leone was full of malice. 'I got a personal report from her yesterday.'

'Oh, I'm so glad,' Miss Barnett twittered as if she hadn't heard a word on the subject of the accident since it happened. 'So sad for him. And for Leone.' She remembered.

'Yes.' He inclined his powerful body in the direction of the older woman. 'That's why Simon has asked me to keep an eye on her.' Abruptly he straightened up, pretended not to notice Leone's simmering silence. 'What about this afternoon? Will the crowds be thronging the waiting room then?'

'Oh, yes. I think it will be quite busy. But,' she smiled up into his face, 'luckily we shan't be on duty then. And I for one am looking forward to putting my feet up. You've no idea just how tiring it can be when you're not used to it.'

'I'm sure it can. But,' his smile was startling, 'I must go along or perhaps Leone will be proved right and Sister Maine will refuse me entry after all.' With a wave of one hand he disappeared, leaving the woman behind the counter in a more confused state than he had found her. If that was possible.

What brought her back to the present was a tiny shuddering sigh, an expression of such blatant yearning that she began to blush for it. Until she realised the sound had not come from her own lips but from Miss Barnett's. And she, poor love, was still looking towards the door through which Gray Ellison had disappeared. There was a moist look in her eye and her lips were slightly parted.

A sudden rush of business prevented them speaking till it was within five minutes of the end of their spell of duty. In fact Leone was removing the sugar from the counter, getting ready to pull down the wire mesh when Miss Barnett said quite suddenly and with a self-conscious little laugh, 'It looks as if your friend found Sister Maine in an amenable mood this morning.'

'He would.' The words spoken so viciously were out before she could stop them, forcing her almost at once to try to soften their impact. 'Simon has told me he can always twist women round his little finger.'

Miss Barnett's smile was faintly uncertain. 'Even Sister Maine?'

'Yes, apparently.' Then switching the conversation, 'If you want to go early, Miss Barnett, then do so. It's nearly closing time and I'm in no particular hurry. Besides it'll only take a minute or two to do the cash.'

'If you're sure.' Miss Barnett often met her sister for lunch on the days she came into town for her hospital duty. 'Then I'll be off and I'll see you in a fortnight, Leone, all being well. Oh, and,' she paused with her hand on the doorknob, 'I hope you find Simon still improving when you see him today.'

'I'm sure I shall.' Busily she began emptying the till. 'I'll tell him you were asking about him anyway.

She had been alone in the shop for only a few minutes, the security grille very firmly down when from the corner of her eye Leone caught sight of a familiar figure hanging about in the waiting hall. Although she gave no sign of having seen him she felt a trickle of nervousness run down her spine. And at the same time there was a contradictory raising of her spirits, almost as if she had been postponing her departure from the shop in the hope of seeing him. Abandoning her excessive wiping of the surfaces she moved out of his sight, rinsed the cloth and after a quick check of her reflection in the mirror behind the door she switched off the electricity in preparation for her departure.

Even when she was locking the door of the shop she contrived to appear unaware of his presence, looking startled as he appeared in front of her as she turned round. 'Oh, hello.' Her tone implied he was the last person she had expected to see and for a second she busied herself unclipping her red cross badge from her neat navy cotton dress, dropping it, with the keys, into her bag as she walked towards the exit.

'How was Simon?' she asked as he opened the swing door for her. 'I presume you found Sister Maine in a docile mood.'

'Simon was fine. Sister Maine unfortunately wasn't on duty today but Sister McDonald had no objection to my visit

'My, my,' she taunted. 'How wonderful to be so popular with the nurses.'

'It helps to be able to get along with people.' They had reached the car park and she was searching for her car keys.

'It was you I came to see more than Simon.'

His words made her look at him properly for the first time since his reappearance. 'Me?' She frowned in mystification. 'I can't believe it.'

'It's the truth.' The stormy look in his eyes contrasted strongly with the cool manner of his statement.

'And why?' Her response to the expression was instant and uncontrollable. 'Why on earth did you want to see me?' At last she found her key, slipped it into the lock with fingers visibly shaking.

'Let me do that for you.' His hand closed on hers, Leone gazed at the interlinking fingers and bit her lip in an effort to stifle the shudder that threatened her. Her mind was filled with recollections of what had happened between them at their last meeting, thoughts of how his mouth had felt against hers made her feel extremely vulnerable. Then she realised that he was locking the car again, withdrawing the key which he held lightly clasped in his hand.

'Do you mind?' The fingers which he had dropped were raised as she asked for the return of her property. 'I'm expected home for lunch.'

'I'm asking you to come with me for lunch.'

Her features assumed an expression of extreme, patronising amusement. 'You can't surely be serious.'

'I told you before,' he was watching her closely and his attention appeared to centre on her mouth more than was absolutely necessary, 'that I seldom say things I don't mean.'

'Well, I'm sorry, but as I told you I'm expected home for lunch so if you would give me . . .'

'I explained to your mother that you might be having lunch with me.'

'You,' her eyes narrowed ominously, 'did what?'

'I went up to Clarewood to see you and your mother told me where you were. She said she would understand if you didn't return as planned.'

'Well, you have a nerve I must say.' Her eyes flashed angrily. 'To tell my mother that I wouldn't be home for lunch because the moment you asked me I should fall into your arms.'

'I didn't say that.' His mouth threatened to break into a smile. 'I merely told her that I thought there was every chance you would accept. Nevertheless, if you do decide to fall into my arms I shall regard it as a bonus.'

'Really. Then I'm sorry you're going to be disappointed on both counts. So if you would please give me the key ...'

'I'll be disappointed if you won't come,' he ignored her contemptuous snort, '*only* because I want to show you the yacht.'

'The yacht?' She was startled.

'Yes, I thought we could have lunch on board and then if you cared to we could go for a sail.'

'Oh ...' Something inside her was weakening. While her mind told her she would be mad to take risks, feeling as she did about this man, there was a wild inclination to test it out, to prove to herself that he meant nothing to her, that the events on the beach were a mere aberration. Instead she insisted, 'I'm going to visit Simon this afternoon. I refuse to disappoint him.'

A dark eyebrow was raised in mocking comment, as if questioning the disappointment Simon might be feeling. 'But he's given you an exeat. He would like me to take you to lunch and then for a sail. Besides,' he drawled 'he asked me to tell you he's going along to physiotherapy at two.'

Angry colour flared into Leone's face and to her horror she found that her annoyance was for her fiancé more than the man beside her. How dared he throw her in the direction of this dangerous stranger? Did he want her to . . .? At that point her thoughts broke off, she found she dared not contemplate what might happen if she went off with Gray Ellison. And yet contrarily she heard herself agreeing to place herself at risk.

'Very well,' she said coldly. 'It seems that between you, the whole thing has been arranged, so I'll go along with it.' Her tone conveyed clearly what she thought of the prospect but naturally he chose to ignore that.

'Good.' At last he held out the car keys to her with a disarming grin. For a moment she considered snatching them, unlocking the door and driving away before he could do anything about it but a look at his expression told her he knew exactly what she was thinking and that he was prepared to use force if necessary to thwart her and to gain his own way. Besides, a scene in the car park amid the constant comings and goings of both staff and patients, was the last thing she was ready to cope with at this juncture. She allowed herself to be led to the car which she remembered so well from the previous night, was settled comfortably in the passenger seat by the time they moved away.

'I can bring you up here to collect your car later. Perhaps you can visit Simon in the evening instead of this afternoon.' His comment did not call for a reply and she took delight in refusing to give one. Instead she sat staring stolidly in front of her but was quite unable to conceal from herself the state of soaring excitement which pervaded her whole body.

It was quiet in the small harbour area when he parked the car close to where the boat was moored, the hot midday sunshine seemed to blanket them in somnolent warmth as they crossed over and mounted the gangplank. Closer to, the vessel was even more impressive than it had been at a distance, much the largest and most expensive-looking craft in the basin at that moment.

And yet Leone found that her interest was less in the *Sea Trekker* or its appointments than in the people who sailed her. In particular the young woman who had made such an impression on the bystanders the other day. And as if on cue a door at the foot of a short stairway leading below opened and she stood there, negligently leaning against an upright, looking at them with a peculiar expression in her striking sea-green eyes.

'Oh, Laverne, come on up will you?'

The girl watched for a few seconds without appearing to have heard the request, then she yawned rather pointedly, showing small perfect white teeth and slowly began to pull herself upstairs, using the rail as a lever. 'Sure,' she said, and as she moved into the full glare of the sun, pulled down from the top of her head a pair of oversized sunglasses.

'Leone, this is Laverne O'Casey. She's the . . . cook on board.' The hesitation before he decided just what her role was made Leone blush. Why, she couldn't imagine. If there was any embarrassment then she ought to have felt it less than anyone. 'Laverne, Leone Chevenix. I've told you about her.'

Still blushing Leone held out her hand but it was a moment before the other girl took it. Contrary to what she had hoped, the . . . cook was as stunning as she had first imagined, even if she was a few years older than the initial hasty assessment had suggested. Her appearance had inclined Leone to imagine she was French, probably the result of a strong resemblance to the young Bardot, everything about her shrieked Cannes but the single word spoken pointed to America. A suspicion almost immediately confirmed when she spoke again.

'Gray was telling me about you.' Apprehension about what that could mean caused Leone to shoot an angry glance towards him but as luck would have it he appeared to have eyes only for his . . . cook. As what man wouldn't? Today the white slacks had given way to navy jeans, tight enough to show every tantalising curve and the red T-shirt was surely calculated to give even the most happily married man an increased pulse rate.

'Really.' She knew her tone was stiff and condescending and chilly, also that for some reason this was welcomed by Miss O'Casey who smiled witheringly.

'Yes. I was so sorry. I should have hated to have my wedding called off at the last minute.' Her tone implied a bride left waiting at the church by an absconding bridegroom.

'It was pretty ghastly.' She turned and strolled to the rail, apparently paying no attention to what was being said, in fact, straining her ears.

'I'm off now, Gray. The meal's all ready in the salon.'

'You'd best hurry if you mean to catch that train. Well, I'll see you when you decide to come back.'

'I expect so.' As Leone turned round she saw the girl bend to pick up a small bag which had been left on one side of the gangway. 'Well, 'bye, Miss Chevenix. Enjoy your trip.'

'Thanks.' Leone's eyes narrowed a little as she

watched the other woman negotiate the gangway and move swiftly along the quayside. There was a jaunty, free-wheeling air about Laverne O'Casey which made her feel stodgy and dull. Sailing about the world with a fascinating man ... She sighed, revealing without realising it, a dissatisfied longing.

'Come on then,' Gray was in front of her, looking down with an intensely speculative expression which she refused to meet, 'let's go inside, shall we? You must be hungry after your long session serving teas and buttered brazils.' He led the way below, settling her into a small upholstered chair while he began to fix some drinks. She heard the clink of ice and realising how thirsty she felt, sipped gratefully before placing the glass on the table in front of them.

'Tell me,' he went on when he had taken the seat opposite her, 'did you really know Simon loves those toffees I took for him today?'

'Of course.' Her heart was hammering in agitation and purely in defence she raised her glass once more, hiding part of her face from his insistent gaze.

'Then, can you explain how it is he told me he can't bear the sight of the things?'

'Oh.' She replaced the glass with a bump.

'Yes. I'm wondering if you were getting your own back on me in some way. Trying to take me down a peg.' He paused and she tried to decide whether he was really teasing. 'I know you think I need it.'

As far as that went she contented herself with raising an eyebrow which could have meant anything but her own curiosity burst out. 'But what did you do with them?' She was all at once longing to laugh.

'Well,' he frowned, 'I did think of bringing them back and asking for my money back but I thought perhaps Miss Barnett would have gone. I fancied my chances with her more than with you. But in the end I decided to go wild. I told Simon to give them to Sister Maine. With my compliments.'

Delight bubbled suddenly up in her veins, dispelling all her angry emotions, speculatively she looked at her empty glass, wondering if the gin and tonic had been especially strong.

'Another?' He drained his own glass and stood up but she shook her head.

'No, I won't, thanks. One is my limit.' And she remembered that one glass of champagne too many had been the cause of much of her present trouble.

'Then I won't persuade you.' He reached out a hand and she allowed him to pull her to her feet, made no attempt to escape the strong arms which circled her. 'And I won't be accused of using alcohol in an attempt to have my way with you.'

'Do you want to?' To her own astonishment she sounded quite flirtatious, coquettish almost. 'Have your way with me I mean.'

For a second or two he looked down at her with an expression that blazed with emotion. 'By God I do.'

But instantly he had released her, had turned away to the far end of the room where a table was set with two places. Leone gazed after him, knowing that his confession, if she could believe it, was what she had longed to hear, more than anything in the world.

'Let's eat,' he said and pulled out a chair for her to sit on.

Whatever other functions she performed on board— even consideration of that matter brought a twist of discomfort to Leone's chest—she had to be fair and admit that the American woman was a good cook. More than that, she had provided an excellent meal.

Chilled vichyssoise appeared from a flask, tasting cool and delicious on a day when the temperature was in the upper seventies. Braised steaks from a casserole, flavoured with garlic and spices were delicious and tender, eaten with green salad and hunks of wholemeal bread. The pudding was a cheesecake with a fresh apricot topping, which she had expected to hear had been bought in a delicatessen but which Gray had aggravatingly insisted Laverne had made the previous evening.

'She must,' Leone had resisted wine till almost the end of the meal then yielding to his persuasions she assured herself she could handle just one glass—it was over the rim of this she looked at him as she spoke, 'be worth her weight in gold.'

'Mmm.' He agreed looking directly into her eyes so she had the overwhelming conviction that he could see straight into her mind, that he was taunting her quite deliberately. 'To Laverne.' He raised his glass and swallowed some wine.

'To Laverne,' she retorted, determined not to show him how she felt. 'Laverne.' Critically she raised the glass to the light, studying the colour through narrowed eyes. 'What a strange name.'

'Like yours.' He agreed calmly. 'I've never known a Leone before.'

'And yours,' she retorted quickly. 'It's scarcely a common first name.'

'Ah, but I can explain that. It was my mother's maiden name.'

'So can I,' she returned hotly. 'I was born in Sierra Leone when my father was vice-consul.' So there, her childish manner implied and she was humiliated by the curve of his lips. Humiliated and fascinated, for she was remembering their effect on her. Remembering and longing for a repeat . . .

'Laverne, I happen to know, chose that name herself. She didn't like the name she had been given so she quite simply changed it. Rather bold if you think of it.'

'I should think,' she stifled a hiccup, 'boldness is one of her strong . . . suits.

'I get the feeling you don't care for Laverne.'

'I neither like her. Nor dislike her.' It was a lie. She disliked Laverne so strongly it was unhealthy but she had no intention of admitting as much to him.

'But then you have a habit of disliking people for no known reason, haven't you, Leone?' As he spoke he came round the table to her, pulled her gently to her feet and into his arms. 'Haven't you, Leone?'

She shook her head, or at least she tried to only it was difficult when she had no inclination to take her eyes from his face. The only relief was that there was no anger in the way he was deliberately emphasising her reaction to him.

'Tell me, Leone.' First he gave her a little shake, then the fingers which had been on her shoulders slid down, circled her slender waist making her draw in a sudden breath and hold it. 'Tell me, do you still dislike me?' The hands moved lower, moulding her hips and thighs to his, making her giddy with the host of emotions which were suddenly tearing at her.

She shook her head slightly, her lips parted in denial for strangely all longing to tease and deceive him had left her. Her eyes were on his mouth and as if he had been waiting for a signal, for the invitation her parted lips had implied, she saw it come towards her. And of its own accord, her whole body melted against the strength of his as he pulled her even tighter into his embrace.

Her skin felt as if it were on fire, where his fingers traced a delicate path, nerves she had not known existed leaped into life, her entire emotional existence was being thrown into such disarray . . . His lips brushed against hers, she struggled with the urge to surrender completely, to raise her hands and link them in his hair, hair that she knew would feel like silk against her skin and . . .

'Why don't you . . .' the tenuous contact ended while she was still dwelling on its pleasures, her eyes shot open, humiliated to find those intense brown eyes regarding her with an expression which mocked them both, '. . . give way to your feelings for once and . . .?'

Anger, anger and disappointment, stabbed at her as she dragged herself from his arms, trying to give an impression of self-control, studiously she studied her tinted fingernails. 'You really are the most arrogant man I ever met. Even Simon didn't. prepare me for such total self-satisfaction.' She looked about her with what she hoped was an air of cool serenity, desperate in her desire to conceal the surging frustration which she had no idea how to control, saw her handbag and stepped over to pick it up. 'I think perhaps it's time to go now.'

'And if I should refuse to let you go?'

'Don't be ridiculous,' she scoffed.

'Oh, but I'm not.' He turned a chair towards him, straddled it, leaning his tanned forearms on the back and looked up into her face with the same sardonic expression. 'I was told by your fiancé to take you sailing and that is what I intend to do.'

'Simon ought to know by now that I'm not prepared to allow him to order my every action.'

'What?' He pounced as if she had stepped into a carefully set trap. 'Not even when he's lying on a bed of sickness? I should have thought, Leone,' his eyes disturbed her with their mockery, 'that if you loved him, as much as you insisted the other night that you did, then you would be happy to fall in with his arrangements to cheer you up.'

'Simon is under a misapprehension in thinking that I need cheering up.'

'Surely not. Surely not when you've just had the worst blow any young woman can endure, your wedding cancelled at the last minute.'

'So long as Simon is going to be all right.' The pious words could not stop the faint colour coming into her cheeks and she knew she need not hope he had missed seeing it. 'After all, it wasn't as if I had been jilted. Simon didn't contrive the accident simply to get out of marrying me.'

'No?' His eyes narrowed fiercely and he rose suddenly to his feet, forcing her to look up into his face. 'But you won't deny that you were relieved, will you?'

'How dare you?' She spoke through gritted teeth but she managed to restrain the hand that longed to slap the self-satisfied expression from his face. 'I don't suppose you've ever been in love so you won't know what it feels like.'

'Oh yes.' He said softly, so softly that a shiver ran down her spine and she gazed at him like a rabbit hypnotised by a stoat. 'Oh yes, Leone.' She did not avoid the hand that came out to link round her neck, obeyed his summons to move a little closer. 'I know all about love.'

'Then why,' in spite of her determination she was unable to conceal the tremor of her voice, 'why are you so anxious about Simon?'

'Simon is a fairly simple chap. No.' He caught her head when she would have jerked it aside. 'I don't mean that in a snide way. His feelings are obvious. He's crazy about you. No, yours are the motives I'm questioning. Why are you marrying him, Leone? And why, if you're so keen on the idea did the postponement come as such an overwhelming relief to you?'

'I simply,' at last she had got some control over her

feelings and decided on a way to deal with this man, 'don't understand what you're talking about. You seem determined to believe what you want and nothing I can say will change your mind.' She hitched her handbag on to her arm, at the same time moving casually away from him. 'Well, I can't be bothered trying, it's of so little interest to me. Thank you for lunch.' She treated him to a brief smile, surprised that she could manage the cool detachment she sought. 'And goodbye.'

'Just a minute.' His bulk blocked her path and she looked up into his face in a way which she hoped would underline her cold disdain, yet she could not be sure that her eyes were not a betrayal of the simmering cauldron of strange emotions which were her inside. 'Or I'll get the idea you're afraid to stay with me.'

'Afraid?' Her eyes went wide in simulated amazement. 'Why on earth should I be afraid?'

'You should be afraid because,' his eyes held hers while his fingers on her bare arms were like live electric wires, 'of the way I feel about you just now.'

Leone drew in a breath on a shuddering gasp. The effrontery of the man, practically telling her he would . . . given the opportunity he would . . . 'The thing is, Mr Ellison, it takes two to tango and I'm not the least bit interested in tangoing with you.'

'Who,' he trailed his fingers till they had found hers, 'who's talking about dancing?' It was clear enough he was laughing at her, even though his mouth was unsmiling there was the gleam of amusement in the brown depths of his eyes. 'But of course if you dare not trust yourself?'

'Oh, I trust myself, Mr Ellison.' Of course she didn't. Not right then with his fingers tracing a delicate path on the inner skin of her wrist, not with her legs so weak that she dreaded the necessity of having to walk from the yacht under her own steam. '*You're* the one I don't trust.' She smiled frostily.

'Oh, you can you know.' His fingers removed themselves so unexpectedly she felt deprived.

'Can I?' She felt she was beginning to sound blustery. 'Even in view of what you just said?' She must be mad, standing here arguing with him.

'I certainly have never had to force myself on a woman.'

'How wonderful for you.'

He shrugged as if modesty forbade him agreeing. 'As I said, you can trust me easily enough. But,' his eyes appraised her lazily, making the colour first flood into her face, then drain away, 'if you feel anything like I do then perhaps you'd be advised to run back home to Mummy and Clarewood.' His tone disparaged both her home and her family.

'How dare you speak of my mother like that.' She spoke automatically while her mind was toying with the pleasurable idea of testing out his theory.

'I didn't realise I was using any special tone but if I was, then I apologise. In fact, your mother and I understand each other very well. She's the emotional kind of woman I like. She's probably forgotten more about love than you've ever known.'

'Why you . . .'

'But look, you'd better make up your mind.' Now he was brisk and efficient throwing her completely, upsetting any arguments she might have mustered. 'We can't keep shilly-shallying all day, if we miss the tide then we'll have the decision taken out of our hands.'

'I've told you what I think,' she snapped back.

'You've spoken a lot of nonsense, Leone.' He grinned devilishly. 'Now tell me what you're going to do. And make the right decision or you'll regret it for the rest of your life. After all, you want to have *some* youthful escapades to tell Simon's grandchildren in the middle of the twenty-first century?

It was then that to her astonishment the cabin door opened and a huge man stepped inside. Remote blue eyes skimmed over Leone before moving on to Gray Ellison.

'Time to cast off, boss, if you want to catch the tide.'

'Okay, Lars,' Gray Ellison never took his eyes from the face of the woman standing in front of him, 'get ready to cast off.' The door closed again and Leone stood rooted to the spot.

'Good girl.' He just touched her cheek with a finger. And a moment later she was watching the cliffs of Heyport slip away from her in the certain knowledge that she had committed the most idiotic indiscretion of her life.

CHAPTER FOUR

SHE was mad to have let him taunt her into forgetting how much she disliked and distrusted him. To think she could have been enjoying a quiet afternoon in the garden of Clarewood, there was that new novel she was anxious to get on with, instead of which she was lying on this bed in his cabin, feeling ghastly and wishing she had known she was such a bad sailor.

It wasn't as if the sea was very rough. Just a bit of a roll he had assured her cheerfully when he brought her a cup of tea half an hour ago. He had stood over her, grinning at her discomfort and looking disgustingly healthy, in the navy guernsey pulled over the white shirt he had been wearing earlier. Healthy and handsome, a combination difficult to resist. She looked with a jaundiced eye at the lock of black hair falling over his forehead, at the attractive colour of the bronzed skin. Every inch the matelot. A retch made her put her fingers to her mouth and, pushing him abruptly aside, she made an undignified dash for the small bathroom adjoining what he was pleased to call the captain's cabin.

Although, Leone thought sourly as she sat on the stool recovering from the bout of nausea, it would have been easy to come to an entirely different conclusion, for the shelves were arrayed with a variety of women's beauty products. There were several famous names, all exotic makes which she presumed were favourites of Laverne. Or other girlfriends. She opened her eyes wide and felt violently sick again. Two minutes later, her eyes carefully avoiding any

71

glance in the direction of the porthole and the rolling sea, she lay down again on the bed and groaned. Why, oh why had she come? Simon! It was all his fault. And yet, she remembered what he had gone through in the last ten days, it was all *her* fault. A few tears slipped down her cheeks.

She must have slept, for when she woke it was to find Gray standing over her, a peculiar expression on his face and another cup of tea in one hand. Realising how totally at a disadvantage she was, Leone struggled upright and sipped the tea gratefully, reflecting that the sight of her now ought to dispel any attraction she might have held for him. The thought, which ought to have given her some pleasure, was not as satisfying as she would have supposed.

'I looked in once or twice,' he stood leaning against a heavy chest of drawers, the powerful legs sprawled in front of him, forcing his not inconsiderable physical assets in her direction, 'and you were sleeping.' Leone bent her head over the teacup, hoping the fall of hair would hide the blush that spread over her features. 'It was the best thing you could have done. Why didn't you tell me you were a bad sailor?'

'Because,' the colour had subsided and she felt confident enough to toss back her hair and glare at him, 'because I didn't know. If I had, mad horses would not have dragged me out on this wild goose chase.' To emphasise the point she put down her cup with a bump and swung her feet to the floor, noticing for the first time that they were rising and falling very gently now on the lightest of seas. 'Are we . . .' she flicked back her long lashes to take a look in the direction of the porthole. 'Have we arrived back home?' Thank goodness the nausea had gone.

'Home, well,' he levered himself away from the chest, put down his cup and held out a hand in her direction, a hand which she took without even thinking about it, 'that depends.' One swift jerk brought her to her feet and close to him. 'I am home.'

'Wh ... what,' Leone tried to pretend she was unaware of his nearness, her eyes concentrating on the forest of masts she could now see quite clearly, 'what do you mean? Where on earth are we?'

'We're in Saint Helier. In Jersey. The Channel Islands.'

'I know where Saint Helier is.' She spat at him. 'All I'm asking,' now there was a wail of consternation in her voice, 'is just why you've brought me here?'

'I thought I had explained that to you.' He gave the impression of patience almost exhausted. 'I brought you here simply because Simon, my oldest friend, asked me to try to entertain you and ...'

'That's not what you said before,' she burst in passionately.

'Oh, take no notice of what I said before. What I've just said is the truth basically. If Simon hadn't made the suggestion, I should have been very reluctant to get involved with you.'

'Really?' Recalling that he was still holding her hands she wrenched them away. 'Then that makes two of us if you can remember. And I would be glad if you would take me back as soon as it can be arranged.'

'Is that what you *really* want, Leone?' He walked away from her, towards the window, 'The seas are getting a bit more frolicksome and while there's nothing I like better than running into a wild wind,' he turned round, caught her expression and laughed, 'I don't think the idea is one that will appeal very much to you. Why don't we decide to make the best of things? I'm quite prepared to take you out to dinner. To please Simon, of course.'

'Damn ...' Only just in time she bit back the name

of her fiancé although the thought still lingered in her mind. What on earth was he thinking about, forcing her into this man's company? It was almost as if he *wanted* her to fall . . . 'Damn,' she said again. 'I have no inclination to have another meal with you but I suppose I've no choice. But . . .' she looked down at her dress which was a trifle crumpled after spending so many hours curled up on his bed, '. . . I can't go ashore looking like this.'

'Oh . . . I don't know.' He surveyed her dispassionately. 'I've seen worse. But I'm sure Laverne will have left something you . . .'

'No,' she said. 'No, thank you. Besides, I should have thought it obvious that her things would not fit me.'

'Mmm.' He pursed his lips. 'I suppose you . . .' his eyes drifted over her slender curves, '. . . are a bit . . .' His expression left little room for doubt over which shape he preferred. 'Well,' he said consolingly, 'we can go and find something. There are plenty of stalls where you can pick up a dress. It's going to be a very hot night, so choose something cool.'

The weather in Jersey was balmy. As soon as she stepped ashore, Leone felt the heat rising from the paving stones and although there was a breeze there was no coolness in it. Before they had walked a hundred yards the navy dress was sticking to her back.

'Down here.' He led her along a narrow street with dozens of shops, open-fronted, offering goods for the tourists who were crowding about in a leisurely buying spree. Leone felt herself being enveloped in the good-natured mood of the crowd and did not pull away from his protective touch on her elbow. It was difficult, impossible, to maintain her prickly relationship with her escort, especially when he was going out of his way to advise her on where she could pick up a comfortable dress.

Most of the shops had their wares hanging up
outside and Leone was at once attracted by the
brilliant colours of some obvious imports from
Greece. On her last holiday in Rhodes they had been
all the rage and appeared equally popular here.

'The colour would suit you,' Gray encouraged when
for the third time she returned to one the colour of
clotted cream. 'Try it and see if it fits.'

It was a cheap thing, costing a fraction of the price
she usually paid for her dresses, but it was undeniably
attractive. Alone in the minute fitting-room, Leone
looked at her reflection in dismay, ran a hand over her
bosom, the tip of her tongue over dry lips. There was
only one thing, with this wide neckline, it was
impossible to wear anything under the dress, straps
looked so ugly ... A few minutes later and she had
stripped off her bra and slip and decided it was an
improvement. Besides it was so much cooler.

Trying not to appear too self-conscious she emerged
from the cubicle, looked at Gray for an opinion
though his brief constrained nod could hardly be
called that. Ten minutes later she had added a pair of
cork-soled sandals to the dress and waited while her
cast offs were bundled into a bag. Gray insisted on
paying for her dress and, reluctant to make a fuss in
the shop she allowed him to have his way, privately
she made up her mind to let him have a cheque the
moment this expedition was over.

It seemed natural for them to link hands as they
wandered round the town, everyone else was doing it
and it would have seemed stuffy to refuse. Besides, it
was a very pleasant feeling to be with a man who
attracted so many sidelong female glances ... And it
was pleasant to catch sight of their reflection in a
darkened window as they strolled along. Leone
thought she would hardly have known herself, she

looked so relaxed, so casual in her flowing midi-length dress.

And he had been right about one thing, both the colour and the style suited her. Whereas this kind of cotton, a mass of minute pleats could tend to make women look a trifle shapeless, in her case it seemed to draw attention to her long slender figure, hinted with intriguing subtlety at warm curves ... The thought caused her to smile and without realising what she was doing, she had relaxed against him, his arm at once coming about her shoulders so she felt warm and safe.

Well, not too safe, she told herself with a faint giggle. Then when he looked down at her with an eyebrow raised questioningly she shook her head teasingly and looked away.

'Seen all you want to of the town?' he asked her after a while and, taking her confirmation more or less for granted, he led her towards a garage and before she knew where she was Leone found herself being driven along a coast road. It was a spectacular drive in the dying rays of the sun, the waves breaking on craggy beaches, the foam tinted pink by the fading light.

Without speaking they drew in for a moment, watched the sunset, a glorious kaleidoscope of green and orange and violet above a sea that was rough enough to serve as a warning for the return trip. On they drove, in a silence that was surprisingly amiable, and after several miles he turned off the main road, bumping and lurching along what was little more than a track, pulling up in front of a large sprawling farm house.

'Now.' He turned and grinned at her, bent to undo the seat-belt catch, coming so close that she became suddenly more aware of the feel of her dress on her bare skin. 'Now,' and his voice sounded slightly husky, as if he was conscious of the same feelings as she was experiencing, 'this really is home.'

In a moment he was round, opening her door and they were walking together over paving stones, old and worn, subtly coloured towards a massive front door which, surprisingly, opened when he turned the handle. The hall was large, dark and cool, smelt of lavender and drying herbs, against the farthest wall was an ancient bench in dark oak and the banisters looked as if they had been there since the middle ages. The floor was tiled in shades of brown and soft dull reds with here and there large rugs in cream wool.

As they stood, Leone admiring and Gray studying her reaction, a door somewhere at the far end of a corridor opened, there was the sound of a woman's footsteps coming towards them. Gray turned, a smile on his face and Leone saw a tall woman, middle-aged and rather attractive, cross the hall.

'Gray, dear.' While she held up her face for his kiss, her eyes were keenly appraising the visitor and she smiled, holding out a hand as the introductions were begun.

'And, Leone, this is my Aunt Meg, Mrs Barnstable.'

The woman's greeting was warm but almost at once she went on to enquire about the kind of crossing they had had, smiled sympathetically when Gray explained that Leone had been seasick.

'The most awful feeling.' As she spoke she was leading them through to a small comfortable room, furnished like a library but with several easy chairs grouped round a coffee table, the french windows were thrown open to admit all the mingling scents of the walled garden. Two of the walls were lined with shelves bearing hundreds of books, opposite the window there was a fireplace, its highly polished brass canopy and fender brightening that wall. It was easy for Leone to imagine how attractive it would look in the winter, flames leaping from apple logs or . . .

'Tea?' Mrs Barnstable's voice interrupted her thoughts. 'Or perhaps it's a bit late for that. Maybe a drink would be better.'

Just as Leone was about to say she would love some tea, Gray butted in. 'Maybe just a drink, Aunt Meg, thanks. We're eating at Jean-Pierre's and don't want to be late.'

But Mrs Barnstable must have seen the expression on the visitor's face for she smiled at Leone. 'Let her answer for herself, my dear. Now, Leone, if you'd like some tea, just say so.'

'Sorry.' Gray grinned, looking for a moment like a small boy caught out in a misdemeanour. 'Of course she'll want tea. That's what one always wants . . .' He allowed his words to drift away as if he were too delicate to mention seasickness.

When they were alone in the room Leone could not help a note of asperity returning to her voice. 'You do seem to have made rather a lot of plans. Your aunt seems to have been more in the picture than I was.'

'Well, I told you.' He, too, sounded irritated and as he spoke he lit a cigarette and glowered at her through the smoke. 'I was trying to help Simon out of a spot. Besides, it is quite easy to ring the Channel Islands you know.'

'I still think you were taking a lot for granted . . .'

'Don't worry, my sweet.' His sudden grin didn't altogether convince her that his annoyance had gone. 'None of it would have been wasted. If you had refused to come, there was a substitute lined up.'

Leone's angry retort was diverted by the arrival of Mrs Barnstable with a teatray which she placed on the table in front of them with a tiny sigh of satisfaction.

'There now,' she handed one of the delicate cups to Leone, 'do have a biscuit if you would like one. But whatever you do don't spoil your appetite for Jean-Pierre's cooking. It really is something rather special.' As she handed a cup to her nephew she asked a question which made Leone splutter slightly. 'And how is Simon?'

'Oh,' the brown eyes appeared to be riveted on the girl's face as he answered, 'he seems to be getting on quickly now but . . .'

'Oh dear, excuse me.' From the direction of the hall a telephone was ringing with some persistence. 'It'll be Phoebe I expect, wondering when I'm coming to pick her up.' A moment later she had disappeared in a whirl of dark printed skirts.

'I get the impression,' Leone put down her cup on the polished surface of the table, 'that your aunt doesn't understand exactly who I am.'

'No?' He raised an eyebrow. 'I thought I had told her who you are.'

'You told her my name. What you don't seem to have said is that Simon is my fiancé.'

'It isn't a secret. You can tell her. If you want to.' If you dare his final words implied and she felt herself colouring in exasperation.

But almost at once Mrs Barnstable came back into the room, talking quickly and apologetically about her friend Phoebe, being late for the bridge session and would Leone please forgive her for rushing away.

'If I had had the least idea that Gray was coming today but of course I didn't know till this morning. You will excuse me, Leone.' She smiled rather breathlessly.

'Of course. I know just how important bridge is.' Leone said ruefully. 'My mother is a devotee.'

'Oh, is she? Well, we must talk about it some time.'

She bustled from the room, reappearing for a second, her head just poked round the door as she said goodbye.

'I hope you enjoy your meal,' now the door was closing on the perfectly coiffed grey head, 'see you both in the morning.' And a second later the sound of the front door banging echoed through the house.

For what seemed like ten minutes but was probably a mere ten seconds Leone sat perfectly still, facing the man on the other side of the table. Now that it was almost dark she could see his head outlined against the deep blue of the sky outside the window and knew he was looking at her. At last the words came but faintly.

'What on earth did she mean by that?'

'By what?' The end of the cigarette glowed as he pulled smoke into his lungs and his features were slightly illuminated.

'You know perfectly well. What did your aunt mean by saying she would see me in the morning?'

'Just that, I think. She expects us both to spend the night here.'

'Why . . .?' Her voice rose slightly. 'Why should she expect that unless she had been told we were staying?'

'You want to return tonight?'

'Of course I want to return tonight. Why do you ask such idiotic questions?'

'I don't see anything idiotic about it. It seems perfectly logical. You haven't been to Jersey before, you told me so. You like it, so why not stay on for a day or two and look around?'

'That is such a stupid suggestion that I'm not even trying to find an answer. Will you please take me home tonight?'

'It's a bit wild, Leone.' She saw him grind out the partially smoked cigarette, then his finger went to a switch which operated a large green shaded table lamp in one corner making it easy for her to see his dark mocking face. 'The return trip will be much rougher than coming across. Do you think you can take it? Twice in one day?'

The very idea was enough to make her blench but she wasn't going to let him see that. 'Of course I can take it,' she snapped. 'But if it's going to be as bad as all that then perhaps we ought to forget about dinner. After all, there's no point in spending money on a meal I'm going to lose between Jersey and the south coast of England.'

'Mmm.' He pretended to agree with her but was having obvious difficulty in hiding his amusement. 'There is something in that. But on the other hand I feel a bit hungry and I'm not likely to be seasick. Come on, Leone,' now he was blatantly cajoling, 'you'd best stay the night here. If you object to the house, then we can always sleep on board. In the harbour I mean.'

Recollection of the small cabin, the intimacy of being there with him brought the colour back to her cheeks. 'Really, I think I had better go home, My parents will be worried if I don't come back.'

'Come on.' With one lithe move he got to his feet. 'I'll show you where you can tidy up if you want then we can discuss the whole thing over dinner.' And stupidly she put her hand into his, allowed herself to be pulled, gently but insistently to her feet. Not quite into his arms although she could have sworn there was a second when that had been his intention. If she was right and it had been, then he changed his mind. He merely stood there, her fingers not yet released by his, looking down at her with that strange expression in his eyes and she got the impression that he was aware of every pulse of her heart, of every throbbing exaggerated beat which robbed her of breath.

Then he turned away, went to the door which he held open for her and without speaking led her up the staircase, carpeted luxuriously yet unobtrusively in a shade that exactly matched the rich sheen of the wood, along a wide corridor, wall lamps reflecting here and there a glow of copper, one or two carefully chosen prints. Then he paused at last before a door, giving her a searching look.

'You should find everything you want. Straight through for the bathroom. Now if you'll excuse me I'll go and change. See you in about fifteen minutes.' A sudden rueful grin made him look unexpectedly boyish as he rubbed his chin. 'I could do with a shave.'

The bedroom into which she walked was luxurious in an understated kind of way, someone had been very careful to keep the modernisation faithful to the age and style of the house. The furniture looked like eighteenth-century French. Leone, although by no means an expert, had trailed round too many antique showrooms when that had been her mother's latest fad, to be wholly ignorant. The satiny surface of a three-drawer commode told her it was a genuine piece but the springs of the bed when tested placed that in the final quarter of the twentieth century. Only, the ceiling height posts and drapes at the head against the wall blended well with the other furnishings.

On the walls which were covered in a light paper with an unobtrusive pattern of delicate flowers, were one or two pictures which, when she moved closer, she could see were embroideries in the finest, most delicate work. At each side of the bed hung still life flower arrangements and a third on the opposite wall was a very attractive sampler. Leone leaned closer, trying to distinguish the words, to assist her eyes she switched on one of the lamps on a side table immediately underneath.

'Marie Violette Ellison aged 10 finish'd this sampler, 4th August, 1845.' Round the edge of the picture was a wide border of small flowers, like the rest of the work completed in cross stitch, at the top was the first verse of the 23rd Psalm, there were several figures grouped about a house and four cherry trees, very upright in spite of being loaded with fruit.

Leone smiled to herself as she thought of the little girl embarking on such a daunting task, the relief she would have felt as she put in the last stitch. And apart from a tiny bit of crowding with a few words, it had been worked beautifully.

In the bathroom, too, she saw that everything had been kept in character, and took pleasure in the rose strewn suite which looked simple and rustic. But she had little time to waste, so washed quickly and then rather regretful of the restrictions placed on her swiftly began to do her face with what she had had in her bag when Gray Ellison effected his clever abduction. The word which had come into her mind made her pause in the act of smearing some colour on to her lips, brought a faint warmth to her face and a confused hammering of pulses. Abduction, how ridiculous could one get? There had been nothing to stop her walking off the *Trekker* before she left England. She was here for one reason only and that was because she had chosen to come. At some time in the not too distant future she must think about that, decide just why she had reached that particular alternative. Surely it couldn't be that her feelings for Gray Ellison had altered in some subtle way. She couldn't . . .

Abruptly she pushed the thought from her mind and turned away from the mirror, switching off the light as she left the bathroom but pausing in front of the pier glass in the bedroom where she could get a more satisfactory impression of her appearance. The dress was lovely. Cheap it had been and maybe it wouldn't wash well but for an evening like this it was absolutely right. Round the neckline was a frill of gold lace matching two on the flounces of the skirt and another round the cap sleeves, there was a tie belt which was a simple length of the material but it cinched her waist nicely and drew attention to the curves above and below. She let out a shuddering, half-excited sigh of satisfaction and on an impulse took out her comb and flicked the ends of her hair, watched them float more distractingly away from her head.

Although just who she expected to be distracted, she could not guess. Yes, the brilliant eyes looked back at her, yes she could. The very same person she hoped would be distracted by the tremulous wide mouth, the sweeping fringe of lashes which she had touched with gilt a few moments earlier. And the reasons for all that could not be analysed at this moment, there just wasn't time. A knock at her door confirmed that the time for introspection had not yet come.

Later would be time enough. Excitement rose in her, making her voice husky and as she picked up her bag she decided she would do nothing to suppress her feelings, she would do precisely what the man had said, enjoy herself and have something to tell her grandchildren in about thirty years. It escaped her mind that it was Simon's grandchildren he had spoken of.

'You want to ring your mother?' By the time she got down he was in the hall, flicking abstractedly through a magazine, confounding her idea that he had watched her descent through those disturbing eyes. But she seemed much more aware of him. Impossible to be otherwise when he looked so devastatingly dark and dangerous. And handsome, her increased pulses would

have told her so if by some mischance her brain had
failed to recognise that fact. Dark slacks emphasised
length of leg and strong powerful thighs, white shirt,
wide-sleeved and open half-way down the chest, she
felt her heart beating in slow powerful strokes against
her rib cage, the spicy scent of cologne rose elusively
in her nostrils to disturb her still further.

She realised he was waiting for a response of some
kind and her eyes flicked towards his, a question in
her upturned face which she hoped would go some
way to concealing what was filling her mind.

'Your mother.' He repeated with a shade of
impatience and his eyes seemed to be all over her,
doubtless amused by the image of awe-struck teenager
she must have been projecting. 'Tell her you have
decided to wait overnight.' He shot back his cuff
giving her eyes time to remark the contrast between
sparkling cotton, skin tanned by wind and sun and a
slim gold wristwatch. 'And then we'd best be off.'

'Oh yes.' At last she forced her numbed tongue to
form a few words. 'Thank you.' It was beginning to
sound as if she had *agreed* to come with him to Jersey.
'W . . . would you get the number for me? Here it is.'
From her handbag she produced a card.

'Okay.' He opened a door and she saw a small room
fitted out like a cloakroom, one or two jackets hung on
the hooks along one wall and in the far corner was a
desk with a telephone. She watched, listened to the
ringing tone before moving and then recognised the
distant sound of her mother's familiar voice.

'Yes, Enid.' He laughed presumably at something
her mother had said and Leone felt her eyes widen in
astonishment. Things must certainly have moved in
the brief visit Gray Ellison had paid to Clarewood this
morning, so much intimacy after such a short
acquaintance, it was unheard of as far as Lady

Chevenix was concerned. She hardly knew whether to resent it or to be amused. The latter she thought, at least while the present awkward circumstances continued. 'Yes, she's here. Wants to speak to you now. Goodbye, see you soon.'

'Hello, Leone.' Her mother seemed not the least bit surprised that she was in the Channel Islands. 'How was the crossing, dear?'

'Oh, pretty awful.' She was conscious of Gray lingering within earshot.

'And you met his aunt. Is she nice?'

'Oh yes. I met her for just a few minutes and she does seem very pleasant.' She was able to imbue her voice with a note of surprise and when she encountered a raised eyebrow turned in her direction, knew that her dig had gone home. But damn him she thought, and how could her mother be so devious, just how long a conversation had the two of them had this morning. 'Mother, will you go and see Simon, tell him I'm sorry, explain what has happened?'

'Of course, darling. And don't worry. I know Simon has been anxious about you and wants you to have a break. Besides, I think he and Gray had all this worked out together and . . .'

'Did they?' Leone asked a little grimly. 'Well I must ask him about that tomorrow when I get back. I'd better go then, Mother. Gray will be growing impatient.' Unreasonably, her tone suggested. 'Goodbye and love to Daddy.'

They were driving along darkened lanes before she spoke and even then she had to force the asperity out of her voice. 'You must have gone to some lengths to plan my abduction.'

'I did go to some trouble to make the arrangements,' he agreed calmly. 'I wouldn't call it abduction myself.'

'Wouldn't you?' she said sarcastically.

'No, I wouldn't.' He had driven off the road and into the courtyard of what looked for all the world like a French auberge, the roof was steeply pitched, overhanging the rows of windows on the upper floors and window boxes spilled glorious splashes of colour down the ivy clad walls. A few discreetly placed lamps cast romantic shadows and that was doubtless why her breathing quickened as he laughed softly and his head came towards her in the semi-darkness. Ostensibly he was releasing her seat-belt but it was hardly a surprise to her when his fingers lingered, then linked round her waist. At once she was still more conscious than she had been of the abandoned underwear, surely it hadn't been all that symbolic ... She herself was feeling no more abandoned than she ever had been, she tried to pretend that her pulses were not racing in mad agitation, impossible when he was now so close that his breath stirred her hair and he spoke so softly that she had to move her head to catch his words. 'You came to me, Leone, of your own free will.'

His mouth was now so close that she knew he was going to kiss her and in spite of all the dire warnings her brain was sending, felt her lips tremble in expectation. And when he came no further, only gazing down at her with an electrifying glitter in his eyes, she was certain he must be aware of her fevered reactions, and of the shaft of humiliation that struck her when she felt him withdraw, humiliation which began to fade only when she was being led through the restaurant by a solicitous young waiter.

The place was crowded, buzzing with talk but in spite of that, one of the best tables had been reserved for them, in a secluded corner with a clear view of the other diners and far enough from the trio playing soft music for the sound to be unobtrusive. In the centre of the room was a small dance floor but so far all the customers seemed to be rather too involved in their meal to be interested.

'Now, Edmond.' Gray's manner with the waiter was so friendly and familiar that Leone understood he must be a frequent visitor and wondered with a curious stab of resentment who his normal companion might be for his evenings at Jean-Pierre's. 'What can you recommend this evening? I have,' he darted a sly look over the top of the menu, 'someone whom I would like to impress.'

'I see.' There was frank admiration in the youth's eyes as he looked at Leone, compensation enough for all the sidelong glances and greetings Gray had received as they walked among the tables. 'Then perhaps *mademoiselle* would care to try the lobster, we have some particularly fine ones today.'

'Mmm.' Gray raised an eyebrow. 'How would that suit you, Leone? Do you care for shellfish?'

'Sounds delicious.'

She listened to the continued consultation, heard instructions given which indicated Gray Ellison knew more than a little about food, nodded at his suggestion for their first course and relaxed as the waiter withdrew after serving them some mysterious aperitif clinking with ice.

'Mmm.' She frowned as she sipped cautiously. 'It's nice. What is it?'

'A particular concoction of Jean-Pierre's. Mainly dry vermouth but with a few secret flavourings. It's one of his specialities. He likes to maintain a great mystique about everything and he's indulged by all his customers, because he's such a character. Edmond, by the way, is his son. Jean-Pierre is French, came to the island just before the war and was deported by the Germans. After the war he came back and married a local girl. For a while he worked in one of the hotels in town but he was able to buy this place about twenty years ago. It was nearly a ruin but he managed to restore it gradually, and now people make day trips from France simply to eat here. He has three daughters who all help in the kitchen and Edmond is the youngest of the family.'

'You seem to know them all so well. I had no idea you came from the Channel Islands.'

'So,' he leaned back in his chair, the glass of golden liquid half-way to his lips, looked at her through slightly narrowed eyes, 'that was one fact Simon did not bore you with.'

'Yes.' Now she was in the mood to play along with him. 'I thought I had been told every boring fact about you, Mr Ellison.' Daringly she rested her elbows on the table, eyes smiled at him over the rim of the glass which she supported in both hands. 'But that seems to have been one he missed.'

If she had hoped for a response to her teasing then she ought to have been pleased for he moved rapidly forward, imitating her pose but without the glass, bringing his face disturbingly close to hers. So close that she was very forcefully aware of the flecks of gold in the brown of his eyes.

'Then perhaps he missed other vital pieces of information.'

With as much coolness as she could muster and that wasn't a great deal, she sipped from her glass, replaced it on the table before returning her chin to her hands and her eyes to his. The second or two had given her time to collect herself, at least . . .

'Perhaps.' She was inclined to leave it there, to give the impression that she had no curiosity about him. 'And that's how I want it to be.' But in spite of herself a half-query just . . . slipped out. 'But I simply can't equate what Simon told me with . . .' she forced herself to look away, casting a leisurely glance over the obviously well-heeled crowd in the restuarant, '... with all this.' Colour flooded her cheeks as her eyes met his, read an expression there which reminded her of just how rude she had been.

'With ...' he drawled hesitantly in a deliberate parody of her own style, '... all what, Leone?' His expression became hard and jeering. 'The possibilities are endless.'

'I ... I ... I'm sorry, it's none of my business.'

'Go on.' The dark eyes were holding hers with a persistent intensity. 'There's something you're dying to know in spite of all your disclaimers.'

'No, really.' It was an effort to look away from him, her gaze fastened on the table-cloth and she drew an eccentric pattern on its smooth surface with a finger nail. Then, absolute relief, Edmond arrived with their first course and she hoped by the time he left again Gray would be prepared to let the subject drop. Surely common courtesy demanded that a matter she found embarrassing should not be pursued. But in spite of all her efforts, her expressions of delight over the leek flan, enthusiasm over the melting pastry, he would not be diverted from the conversation she was now finding so awkward.

'Am I right in supposing that you were going to ask how it was that I,' his lips twisted into a smile that was only half-amused, 'a mere scholarship boy, with no visible means of support, should find myself living a life of comparative luxury?'

'Well,' although her inclination was denial she felt he would not be particularly easy to convince, 'well, yes. I ought not to have asked.'

'But yes, feel free.' The note of biting sarcasm made her catch her breath. 'I'm sure you did it all the time back in Heyport, ask your acquaintances how they came by their money.'

She swallowed the last piece of tart and placed her fork carefully on her plate before looking up at him. 'Do you come here often?' She raised a sophisticated eyebrow and felt relief course warmly through her veins when after a moment, the frown left his face, his eyes sparkled suddenly and he smiled.

The smile, the sudden change from disapproval to amusement caused her heart to give an unexpected lurch, to pause for an instant before rushing on in wild exaggerated pleasure. She raised her glass and drank, then realised it was the wine causing such erratic behaviour, it was alcohol which was coursing so madly through her veins.

'Forgive me.' Until he captured it, she had forgotten that her hand was lying invitingly on the cloth. 'I'm still a touchy blighter.' His finger moved idly against the inner skin of her wrist and he gazed into her eyes. 'Forgive me,' he said again but speaking so softly her whole body melted towards him, unable to reply but hoping that her eyes would tell him that of course she forgave and hoped he would do the same . . .

They had finished the lobster which was so delicious as she had been led to expect and she was mopping the last trace of delectable sauce from her plate with a morsel of bread when he returned to the theme he had found so disturbing.

'Would you believe it if I told you I had made a fortune smuggling drugs from the Middle East?'

'No.' Her response was instant and passionate, surprising herself. 'No,' she repeated more rationally. 'Of course I wouldn't believe it.'

'Why not, Leone?' He leaned forward, took her fingers in a loose grasp as he had done several times during the meal and scattering to the winds her determination to keep her relationship with this man on an even keel. It required the merest friction between his finger and her skin to inflame all the feelings about which she had known nothing. Until ... 'Why not?' His finger moved. ... Until recently.

'Because,' there was barely a quiver in her voice, she hoped her eyes were equally obstructive, 'I don't think you're the kind of man to trade on other people's misery and degradation.'

'Really?' The raised eyebrows were self-mocking. 'Then you do think I have some redeeming features.'

'One or two, maybe.' It was impossible not to smile. And yet, what might that tell him when he was watching her like a hawk?

'Your faith is touching. Lots of people do it you know.'

She waited.

'But you're right.' He released her hand, leaning back in his chair again. 'Nothing so way out as drugs I'm afraid. You know I studied engineering at Cambridge? No?' He grinned his disbelief. 'I thought Simon would have told you. But maybe that was too boring even for Simon. No.' He caught her hand again. 'I didn't mean it like that. Do you know that your eyes change colour when you're mad. No? I thought he might as least have told you that. But of course you're never angry with him so perhaps he doesn't realise ...'

Firmly she withdrew her hand, leaning back in her chair so she was less accessible. 'You were saying something about engineering ...'

'Oh yes,' with a dramatic gesture he put his hand to his forehead. 'Oh yes, I remember now. Well, I had always been keen on sailing, spent most of my childhood pottering about in boats round the island and it was always an ambition to go in for marine engineering. Then, just by chance, I developed a certain kind of injection jet for engines in small craft, no one on this side of the Atlantic was interested so I took it to the States and sold it to one of the major manufacturers. It's being manufactured under licence all over the world and I get a royalty on each one that's sold. All going well, I'll be reaping the rewards well into the middle of the next century.'

'Your children and your grandchildren.' She couldn't have said what made her come up with such an irrelevant comment.

'As you say.' If he had any thoughts on her words then he was keeping them to himself for he continued his story. 'Sheer luck, of course, but then that plays a large part in all our lives, doesn't it? Anyway, it enabled me to buy the farm and part of the land goes down to the sea where there's a small natural harbour. I have one or two other ideas and I plan to develop some of them here. Actually, the trip from South Africa was really a test run for some other things I'm trying out. So far most have functioned well but there are a few snags that want ironing out. I'm not hoping for anything as successful as the Ellison jet,' he grinned, reminding her of the charm which he had in abundance, 'I'm grateful for what I've been able to do so far.' Quite unexpectedly he stood up 'Dance with me?'

Leone stared back at him. It was a question she had hoped he would not ask. While the other diners had been moving round the small intimate floor she had kept her eyes firmly averted, determined that no longing glance in their direction would give him the mistaken idea that she would like to join them. And if he did ask, then she would refuse. Quietly but firmly she would tell him she preferred to sit and talk. Anything, *anything* but risk having his arms about her.

She found herself being led unresisting to the centre of the room, his arms were about her, her head drooped on to his shoulder.

CHAPTER FIVE

'J'attendrai, le jour et la nuit,
J'attendrai toujours ton retour . . .'

THE pleasing light tenor voice crooned into the microphone encouraging Leone to raise her heavy eyelids to glance at the small stout man whom until then she hadn't seen. She was feeling languorous with all that food and wine, the music too had had its effect, she was determined to rationalise the feelings which she couldn't really explain.

'That,' a mouth close to her cheek moved, 'is Jean-Pierre.' The tip of his tongue scorched her skin. 'He sings as well as cooks. But not as well, if you know what I mean.'

Leone giggled, felt herself gathered even more closely and lost all sense of time till Jean-Pierre's voice took up another song, this time seductive French giving way to atrocious English which robbed the occasion of some of its romantic atmosphere.

Forced to try to lip-read she encountered from Jean-Pierre such a boldly lecherous look from shining dark eyes that she at once turned back to Gray for an explanation.

'What on *earth* is he singing?'

'He's saying,' Gray held his head back, looking down at her with a glance that caused a rush of feelings inside her, a glance that took in the drift of her sable dark hair, held her eyes for a heart-stopping minute, lingered over her mouth for an eternity, 'just exactly what I'm feeling at this minute.' His eyes flicked to where the warm swelling curve of her breast could be discerned at the low neckline of her dress.

'I . . .' She was disturbed more than she would have cared to admit at any normal time, disturbed by the intensity of that sliding glance, disturbed, unwittingly longing for that disturbance to continue, to increase and—somehow she was uncertain what she meant—to fulfil all the unexpected feelings she was experiencing. 'I don't . . . understand.' She spoke so softly that he had to bring his head closer. Might that have been her aim, the freshly shaven cheek brushed against hers?

'Some other time,' his voice was deeper than Jean-Pierre's and surprisingly tuneful, 'I could resist you. Some other time, not now.'

Leone's sharply indrawn breath owed more to the words than admiration for his musical abilities although there was no question about the potency of the combination. But the words were such an echo of her own feelings . . . such a dangerous echo . . .

'Shall we,' she spoke with a determination to end the absurd emotion which was developing between them, 'sit down.' And without waiting for his reply she released herself from his arms and returned to the table.

While Gray ate some cheese—she had refused that course—she tried to convince herself that she was interested in what was going on about her. It was one way of pretending she was the cool calm Leone Chevenix whom she wanted to be. She even made one or two casual remarks about what was happening round them, pretended not to see the knowing glances sent to their corner by Jean-Pierre as he embarked on some Italian songs.

'Do you think,' it was impossible to keep the amusement from her voice, 'his Italian is better than his English?' And she was pleased when she saw

Gray's slightly grim expression relax, his lips curved reluctantly.

'It's got to be better, don't you think?' He finished his cheese and wiped his mouth with the napkin but all the time he was looking at her in a way that kept her blood at fever heat. It even flashed into her mind that *he* was a little paler than usual, as if he too were struggling against the feelings that stretched so tautly between them. At least—panic invaded her and she wrenched her eyes away from his—she *hoped* he was fighting those feelings for she couldn't do it *all* on her own.

'Thank you, Edmond.' She tried to transfer her attention to the waiter as he placed a glass of sugared strawberries in front of her but that was a futile gesture for it was impossible to be other than acutely aware of the man sitting opposite her. And she ate the delectable Alpine berries as if they had been purchased from the local supermarket.

He didn't suggest they dance again, an omission which she resented even while trying to pretend it was a relief to her. Conversation faded a bit, too, but each time she snatched a glance in his direction it was to find Gray's eyes intently upon her, a situation she could not accept with the cool disdain she sought.

But at last it seemed time for them to go and as they threaded their way through the now rapidly emptying restaurant they were waylaid by Jean-Pierre, who advanced towards them like some plump little pouter pigeon, a male of the species fully confident of his power to attract any mate he selected.

His brilliant, bold eyes told Leone exactly who he would like to choose for that role. 'Monsieur Gray . . .' He bowed briefly while saving his especial glances for the girl. '. . . You 'ave enjoyed the meal?'

'The meal was, as usual, delicious, Jean-Pierre.'

Harlequin Romance Free Gifts–Free Prizes

38786

WIN A GREAT PRIZE

YES I'll try the Harlequin Preview Service under the terms specified herein. Send me 4 free books and all the other FREE GIFTS. I understand that I also automatically qualify for ALL "Super Celebration" prizes and prize features advertised in 1986. I have written my birthday below. Tell me on my birthday what I win.

▲ If you are NOT signing up for Preview Service, DO NOT use seal. You can win anyway.

FILL IN BIRTHDAY INFORMATION BELOW

MONTH | | DATE | |

this month's featured prize—a dozen roses + 12 $100 bills on winner's birthday + as an added bonus lovely 14k birthstone earrings for 101 other winners.

116 CIR 6003

PLEASE PRINT

NAME

ADDRESS | APT #

CITY

STATE | ZIP

If card is missing write
**Harlequin
"Super Celebration"
Sweepstakes**
901 Fuhrmann Blvd.
P.O. Box 1325
Buffalo, NY 14269

Harlequin
"Super Celebration" Sweepstakes

901 Fuhrmann Blvd.
P.O. Box 1867
Buffalo, NY 14240-1867

PLACE
1ST CLASS
STAMP
HERE

'And, *Mademoiselle?*' The dark eyes rolled encouragingly.

'Yes.' A strong warning hand on her arm subdued her inclination to giggle. 'It was a wonderful meal, Jean-Pierre. And I must congratulate you on your singing as well. It made the evening quite perfect.' Too late she regretted that admission to the tall man standing beside her.

'Ah yes, for Monsieur Gray,' they had reached the door which he held open for them, 'always I try to make the evenings perfect.'

'I'm sure you do.' His words had reminded Leone of what she was about and she tried to shake herself free.

'And how is Mademoiselle Laverne?' Jean-Pierre's words followed them and this time Leone did manage to pull herself away.

'She is fine, Jean-Pierre, thank you. Good night.'

'Good night *Monsieur. Mademoiselle.* Please to return soon.' And the heavy glass door swung closed.

'I get the impression,' they were on their way before she spoke and even then it was difficult for her to conceal the blazing anger the restaurateur's last words had engendered, 'that you do this kind of thing quite often.' How could she have made herself so cheap, to become one more name on a long list which included Laverne O'Cascy?

He waited till he had negotiated a particularly sharp bend before replying, and then his tone was extremely laconic. 'What kind of thing had you in mind?'

In the darkness she felt her skin burn. What *did* she have in mind exactly? That was a question for her even more than for him. So far very little had happened between them that couldn't have been viewed by a maiden aunt, and wasn't she being just a bit stupid and nervous in thinking the evening would end in . . . oh she wasn't even going to think about what she had meant. 'Just what I said,' she returned crisply. 'This kind of thing. Bringing girls over from the mainland, wining them and dining them.'

'No, not often.'

'Just Laverne.' It wasn't very clever to bring that up now, she realised the implication he would put on the words the moment they were uttered, when it was much to late to withdraw them.

'Laverne.' His laugh was brief and almost convincing. 'But I told you she had joined the company as the ship's cook and . . .'

'Yes, you did say,' she butted in sarcastically.

'And Jean-Pierre probably just brought up her name in an attempt to make you jealous. That is how his fairly simple mind would work.'

'Jealous?' Was she perhaps overdoing it, she tried to smooth the indignation from her voice, replace it with amused disdain. 'Why on earth should I be jealous?'

'I haven't the faintest idea.' They had turned into the drive of his house and drew up in front of the main door. Behind panes of glass lights gleamed softly and when he opened the door for her, all the sweet scents of the evening enveloped her like a cloud, stirring her senses. 'I haven't the faintest idea.' He repeated his words as his hands came out to take hers, pulling her to her feet. 'But I hope,' his voice deepened, became husky, 'I hope that he succeeded.' The words, the tone sent a flicker of fire through her veins.

For a moment she couldn't even speak, she would have been content to stand there forever, his hands holding hers but loosely, as if determined to make no demands, yet with his eyes blazing down masterfully, in an attempt to bend her to his will.

She shook her head, the words lingering in the air

about them had to be denied although she could barely remember their content, some basic instinct of self-defence persuaded her that she must.

'Leone.' His head was so close that his breath was on her skin, she felt it stir her hair. She turned her face upwards with a tiny murmur and surrendered her mouth with a sigh that was part regret but mainly a flow of unutterable joy that flooded her body. This was a moment she had dreamed of, had waited for with impatience since ... since those ecstatic bewildering moments spent on the beach that first night, she had dreamed of those moments sleeping and waking. Suddenly her reservations seemed childish, as irrelevant as her tepid feelings for Simon, and she was wildly excited.

Fire surged in her veins for as long as his mouth remained in possession of hers, subsiding marginally when lips moved to her cheeks, leaving a tantalising trail across her closed eyelids, down her throat and she pressed her body against his in a fever of longing.

'Darling.' His voice throbbed and she knew she would never forget the moment he first used that endearment. 'Let's go.' And she allowed herself to be led in through the door, up the long flight of stairs which seemed to take for ever as they paused to touch each other's faces, to tease, to caress, to kiss with increasing urgency.

It was only when the door of her bedroom was pushed open that she realised how far they had come but then his mouth was again on hers, depriving her of thought, drugging in its unbearable sweetness. Her body shuddered in delight, her fingers of their own accord twisted themselves in his hair.

Just for a moment a shred of sense, of reason, forced itself into her mind and she heard herself reminding him of his aunt.

'What?' He was pushing her back on to the bed, she felt the support of downy pillows as she looked up into his face in the near darkness.

'Your aunt.' It was the merest whisper and she did not resist the fingers pulling at the ties of her neckline. 'She might have heard.'

He laughed hoarsely. 'Don't worry. I may have forgotten to say, she doesn't live with me. Just keeps an eye on things when I'm away. There's no one in the house but ourselves, darling.'

And Leone, who ought to have felt anger and indignation was instead filled with an overwhelming relief that Mrs Barnstable could be wiped from her memory, she could give herself up to the pleasures of the moment. The dress was pulled from her shoulders and she felt the touch of his mouth on her breast as delicate and seductive as a butterfly's wing. And instinctively she slipped her hands in the open front of his shirt, unable to deny the urges which had been tormenting her all evening. She found it an even more entrancing experience than she had imagined, for both of them it was a delight to her to discover as he caught at her hands with a groan, held them still.

He parted from her briefly then, looking down at her as he struggled with cufflinks.

'Help me.' He held them out to her and she sat up, fingers clumsy in their impatience then she lay back, heart throbbing as she saw the shirt wrenched off and consigned to a far corner of the room. Then, another desolate thought struck her, so when his arms came possessively round her again she rubbed her cheek against his, murmured in his ear.

'What? Never?' And there was such incredulity in his voice that she felt a moment's panic. She knew about men. At least ... she had heard of their

preference for women with experience. 'Do you mean
Simon never . . .?'

'No, never.' She almost sobbed. Especially not
Simon. And the reason for her abstinence was surely
obvious. She had been waiting for this. For him. And
if he couldn't see that then . . .

'Darling.' A new tenderness was in his voice. 'I'm
glad.' He was slow and gentle when that was what she
wanted. But finally taking her with such passion that
she knew she would never want any other man.

For a few minutes in the dawn she lay, looking at the
dark face on the pillow beside her. She was filled with
a kind of wondering delight as she relived every
moment since they had closed the door of the bedroom
last night, it was an experience for which she had been
wholly unprepared, one which she had welcomed with
both hands once she had recognised the inevitability,
the *rightness* of it. Without thinking she gave a tiny
sigh, put out a hand to touch his cheek, found her
hand immediately captured and held close to the soft
hair on his chest.

She blushed when she realised how closely the dark
eyes were watching her, for how long? she wondered
before she smiled.

'Leone.' The dreamy wonder in his voice echoed
her own feelings, yet there was something in his tone
which stirred her balmy thoughts, brought the blood
back to her cheeks, lips parted to ease the hurrying
breath. 'Regrets?'

It was a moment before she understood, then her
instinct was a passionate shake of the head, a murmur
of protest. 'No . . .' Her free hand drifted over his
chest, she wondered again how a man's body, so hard
and powerful could feel so warm and silky. 'No. Oh
no. No regrets.'

'Don't.' As her hand moved against his skin she felt a shudder rack his body, rejoiced in the sense of power it gave her to disregard his pleas. 'Don't do that, darling, unless . . .'

'Unless?' she cajoled, surprising herself. She had never been the coy flirtatious type but then, until now she had never been in a situation offering quite as many opportunities.

'Unless,' he had captured both of her hands in his, pressing them, palms down against his chest, 'you are prepared for the consequences.' Then his hands circled her waist and for an endless moment he looked down at her, without speaking, motionless except for the rapid rise and fall of his breathing. 'Leone.' His mouth just touched hers, kisses drifted over her cheeks and eyes as he murmured all the endearments she had ever dreamed of hearing from the man she loved. But soon time and sense and coherent thought were shattered as each pulled the other still closer, she felt the sweet tormenting fire in her veins, abandoned herself to the fulfilment which now at last she knew could bring such soaring, undreamed of joy.

Leone sang softly to herself as she lay in the warm scented water in the bath. It was almost nine and she couldn't remember the last time she had slept so late but then, her face coloured, the song died on her lips and was replaced by a rueful little laugh, she hadn't actually slept so very much.

A knock on the door took her sinking down beneath the bubbles, she tried frantically to revive the dying foam but . . . 'May I come in, Leone?'

'Yes.' She tried to pretend she was used to this situation, to having men come and inspect her in the bath but knew she had failed when he noticed the pinkness of her cheeks and laughed.

'I thought you would like some tea.' He carried a

small tray with two cups, one of which was handed to her while he balanced himself on the edge of the wash hand basin, surveying her with slow appreciation. 'I'm glad to see you don't wear a shower cap.'

'Oh.' Leone was wondering how she could drink tea while in this half-submerged situation. 'I had to improvise and pin up my hair.'

'You look beautiful.' Suspicious of him teasing she looked at him keenly but his face was completely serious. And there was an expression on it which sent a pang of almost unbearable bitter-sweetness through her. And it was difficult not to be throbbingly aware of how good he looked himself.

There was something special, specially intimate about seeing a man fresh from his morning shower, hair still damp, slicked down but springing up in little tendrils as it dried. And he looked so effortlessly elegant dressed even as now in the most casual of clothes, a loose towelling T-shirt, cream-coloured, linen slacks the pale brown of freshly baked biscuits, bare feet thrust into espadrilles.

'Drink your tea, Leone.' Over the rim of his cup the dark eyes teased. 'Or I'll think you don't like it.'

It was surprising how easy it was to slip into the role of abandoned woman, she found herself sitting up in the bath, Gray moving to perch on the edge, trailing seductive fingers down her spine while she drank her tea. And when then she stood up she was wrapped in a huge fluffy bath sheet gathered to him regardless of water splashing on to his clothes.

'You're mine now. You know that, don't you?' His voice was urgent against her cheek and any will to disagree with him quickly ebbed, though she doubted its existence in the first place. And with the responses of her own body so insistent, she gloried in being asked such a question.

'Yes.' Thoughts of Simon didn't even trouble her. 'Oh yes.' She assured him, but didn't just then have the confidence to demand an equal commitment from him.

'I'll tell you what we're going to do.' He held her away from him, looked down into her eyes and with one finger traced the sensitive outline of her lips. She longed to feel his mouth against hers but was forced to make do with the sound of his voice, certainly he was making plans that she had no wish to go against. 'We're going to have breakfast first and then we're going into Saint Helier. I'm going to be busy at the *Trekker* for a couple of hours, checking we have plenty of provisions and you can go and buy yourself whatever you need for a couple of days on board.'

'On board?' She couldn't think what he was speaking about, not when his hands were sweeping aside the towel, tantalising her skin with his touch. And yet . . . a couple of days on board . . . memories of the previous day's sail had not been totally obliterated.

'Don't worry, my sweet.' White teeth flashed suddenly. 'We shall be keeping inshore and today the sea's as quiet as a mill pond. But there's a gorgeous isolated cove a few miles away, the kind of place you can reach only by boat and I think we could enjoy ourselves there for a bit.'

'Oh!' The prospect was so entrancing that she could think of no objection yet felt ashamed when he brought up the subject which she *ought* to have considered immediately.

'And just to clear things up, you'd better ring home and let your mother know . . .'

'Oh, I can't.' She thought of Simon lying in hospital and was stricken with guilt. 'I must go home.'

'You're coming with me.' There was just a suggestion in his tone which told her he was quite

capable of taking her with him by force if necessary
and Leone, trying to be honest with herself, knew she
could not go back to Heyport, not just yet. 'Oh and,'
Gray turned to the door of her bedroom, 'don't think
when you come downstairs you need feel embarrassed.
Lots of people come and go in this house and Jeanette
is quite used to it. She's the girl who comes in to clean
each day, you'll like her and she'll have breakfast
ready now.'

He was right about that. Leone did like Jeanette, the
girl from the village, plump and plain, not more than
twenty and with quite a lot to say for herself. Most of
her conversation with Gray was island gossip,
delivered in the slightly peculiar local accent, difficult
for unaccustomed ears so Leone was pleased when at
last she and Gray were left alone together to enjoy the
delicious rolls, rich with yellow butter and cherry jam
and drink strong black coffee from the large china
cups.

It was another glorious morning and Leone enjoyed
eating at the open windows, hearing waves break on
the shore which was just out of sight. Through a
screen of tall trees she could see the sparkle of brilliant
water, gulls wheeling and screaming over it.

They were driving into town, she making a mental
list of the things she must buy when Gray spoke of the
telephone call she had made just before leaving. 'Your
mother didn't mind?' He took his eyes momentarily
from the road, flicking a warm glance in her direction.
'Your staying on I mean.'

'No.' There was surprise in her laugh and she
shrugged. 'No, for some strange reason she didn't. I
thought there would be all kinds of objections but
there were none. In fact she seemed too involved in
her own plans, she and Daddy are going up to
Cumberland for a week.'

'What about Simon?' The note in his voice was slightly bitter.

'He seems to be fine. Oh, Gray, I feel so guilty.'

They had reached the garage where he had picked up the car the previous day and he slid into a parking space, switched off the engine and turned to her. With one hand he captured her chin and held it, forcing her to look up into his face while he stared down with a strange expression. Possessive? Concerned? Determined? Perhaps all of these but something else, too, a hint of resentment maybe. But when he spoke his voice was calm and assured as ever.

'Don't be.' About him was such an air of confidence that all her worries began to dissolve and when his mouth brushed against hers they were simply forgotten. 'Don't be,' he whispered. 'This,' there was a world of meaning in his voice that made her heart race, 'all this is right for us at this moment.'

In the next hour Leone acquired bikinis, shorts, matching tops, a track suit for chilly mornings and it was impossible for her to resist another dress like the one she had worn the previous evening. This time she chose one in deep violet, the cotton gathered on to an embroidered yoke and supported by narrow straps which looked good against her tanned shoulders. She also got some undies, a rather expensive nightie, with a figure-hugging top in white lace and skirt of sheer chiffon. In fact it was so much like one her mother had insisted on her having for her trousseau that Leone blushed as the assistant watched her write out the cheque to pay for it.

Tooth brush, toilet accessories, some face lotions and a small flagon of her favourite perfume, well it was a shame not to take advantage of excise free goods when they were available. She was just emerging from one of the stores, struggling with all her packages when a hand came over her shoulder and a voice murmured in her ear.

'Let me help you. I said buy a few things, not the whole of Saint Helier.'

'Oh, Gray.' Her eyes told him how glad she was to see him and there was something about the lingering expression in his which suggested it was mutual. 'There were quite a few things I thought I must have. I only hope I haven't forgotten anything.'

'If you have, then you'll have to do without. I refuse to break into our precious time together to come back for a pot of face-cream.'

'Is it?' One word seemed to stand out in all those he had spoken. 'Is it that, Gray?'

'What?' For a moment, regardless of the holiday crowds surging about them, he held her close, making her aware of how much she needed him. 'What do you think?' He paused and his eyes raked her face. 'I think in years to come we'll look back on this as the most precious time. Not,' he released her slowly and grinned, 'that I mean it to be the last.'

And as they strolled hand in hand along the quayside, Leone felt like singing. She was happier then she had ever been in her life before. There was just a moment's disappointment when she saw Lars pottering about on deck as they reached the yacht. But then when he immediately made it clear that he was itching to be off, Leone felt she could afford to be more friendly towards him and said her goodbyes with a cheerfulness which contradicted her coolness a moment earlier. While he, with a knowing lop-sided grin allowed his eyes to roam appreciatively before, with a sketchy gesture that might have been a salute, running down the gangway and being swallowed up in the crowds.

As she lay against the rails, watching Gray's skilful

negotiation of the busy harbour, Leone could not quite suppress her feeling of apprehension at the prospect of the open sea. True there wasn't even the slightest of swells visible, the air was so still that the sails remained furled and they were totally dependent on engine power but ... One wave hit the prow as they headed south-east but that was merely the wake from a passing pleasure steamer, Gray grinned at her from the cockpit, made a sign which was so reassuring that she relaxed. And as they continued their coast-hugging route round the island she was delighted and just a bit complacent to find she was suffering not the slightest twinge of squeamishness

After a bit she went below to fetch a book from the cabin which it had been taken for granted she would share with Gray. She was honest enough to admit that any other course would have been shattering. Now, she allowed her eyes to rest on the neatly made bed, fresh sheets from yesterday. *Yesterday.* For heaven's sake was it only yesterday? Smooth dazzling white cotton folded back over a blanket of brilliant blue. She sat on the edge for a moment, smoothed a hand over the pillow where she imagined later his head would lie. Then in a fever of emotion pressed her face into the cool cloth and *willed* the hours away. But when she went up on deck she sat reading, turning pages with every indication of composure.

If there was such a place as heaven on earth, surely this untouched corner miles from anywhere was it. There was at least a mile's dazzle of pure white sand backed by towering cliffs and jutting out at each end of a crescent into a sea as smooth and glittery as blue glass. Leone identified it the moment it was pointed out to her from the deck of the *Trekker*, leaning over the rail and trying to discern exactly where the long brown finger was indicating. It was difficult, her eyes behind dark glasses were suddenly too blurry to focus, Gray laughed, pulled her closer, his head against hers as he insisted she should find the place he was showing her.

And then suddenly he turned her round to face him, giving her a little shake of impatience, still smiling but his expression altered as he looked down at her. And in an attempt to conceal her highly emotional state she rubbed noses with him and linked her arms about his neck and they kissed, his mouth exploring hers with all the tenderness a lover was allowed.

'You know, if you keep this up we might never reach shore.' His voice was husky, exciting still further the yearning she had for him.

'Would that matter so much?'

'It might just.' He seemed to snap out of the mood and his grin was self-mocking. 'If we found ourselves aground on some rocks. The coast about here has its dangers. Even on a day like this. And I should hate to have to radio for assistance.'

'All right then.' Reluctantly she let him go. '*I* should hate to be the cause of your embarrassment.'

'In the meantime, maybe you feel like going along to the galley and knocking up something to eat. I suppose you can cook.'

'Reasonably well. I did all the right things you know, went to a cookery school for a bit.'

'In expectation of marrying someone who would want you to entertain for him.' They were sitting on the warm sand of the Real Cove, eating the picnic she had prepared when he came back to the subject of her training and there was an edge to his remark that put her at once on the defensive.

'Most men expect their wives to do that.'

'But didn't you ever want to do something more?'

The brown eyes flashed at her with something like animosity.

'More?' she drawled, but with a pang that the mood between them seemed to have become just a bit edgy.

'Yes. You're bright enough and . . .'

'Oh, thank you.'

'And,' ignoring her faint sarcasm he continued, 'I should have thought you would have wanted to stretch yourself a bit more. I'm sure you could do something more fulfilling than help in the Red Cross shop.'

'I do have other interests you know.'

'Such as . . .?'

Her mind raced feverishly. 'I used to paint a little. Besides . . .'

'Besides . . .'

'Oh, you wouldn't understand, so why should I explain.' Tears were stinging behind her eyes and she refused to look at him. Why should she make excuses for what had at the time been as much of a disappointment to her . . .

'Why do you think I wouldn't understand?' His voice was quiet now, and gentle. 'All I'm asking is why you chose the *cordon bleu* course, that's what all the debs, unfit for anything more demanding do, the ones who hope to marry into the House of Commons. Why didn't you go to university?'

'I could have.' She bit her lips. 'And I meant to. In fact I was accepted by London. But my mother became seriously ill just before and I had to stay at the Embassy, we were in Bangkok at the time and she wanted me near her. After that, when she was better again, it seemed too late, all my friends had moved on and I didn't fancy being the oldest student in my year. So, that's why I did the *cordon bleau*. And in spite of what you say it wasn't filled with empty-headed debs. Quite a lot of older women

were in the class and some of the girls are now
making a living out of catering.

'No regrets?' It was what he had asked her this
morning in an entirely different atmosphere, the idea
that he hadn't remembered struck her like a blow and
strengthened her reaction accordingly.

'Of course I have regrets.' Angrily she faced him.
'Isn't that what life's about? Regrets. I . . .' The tears
were now too close for her to say that the regrets
would have been more if she had ignored her mother's
wishes.

'Leone.' He caught her, pushing her back on to the
hot sand where she lay staring up at him, torn between
resentment and the weakness caused by the slightest
contact between them. 'Darling. Don't be upset, I was
asking only because I have to know everything about
you. You see,' the firm lips curved, the eyes sparkled
in self-mockery, 'I'm wildly jealous of the years when
I didn't know you. But I was clumsy in the way I
expressed myself. Forgive me,' he said very softly.
And with his finger tracing the line of her chin,
trickling down her throat, what choice did she have?

'Now I suggest,' with what seemed like a
determined effort he held her a little way from him,
'you get into your bikini and we'll swim. Or if you
prefer it . . .' he allowed his eyes to drift over the
feminine contours outlined by her T-shirt, '. . . it is
the most private spot in the world.'

'I don't prefer it.' She laughed and rolled away from
him, enjoying the side play in the intense relationship
which had developed between them so joyfully. 'I do,'
she got to her feet and stood laughing down at him
confident that the white shorts showed off her long
and lightly tanned legs to their best advantage, 'have
some modesty, you know.' Unlike Laverne she assured
herself privately. But then the expression in Gray's

eyes reminded her of certain things which put her
confident statement into question, she blushed and
yelled as a hand snaked out to grasp her ankle.

'But maybe I prefer it.'

'Then *you* will just have to get used to doing
without.' But she knew her eyes were shining, giving
him an entirely different message.

Leone had always been a powerful swimmer,
entirely at home in the water, she had even done a
little skin-diving, so when Gray brought the masks
from the yacht they were able to begin some
underwater exploration of the rocks and caverns that
circled the cove. Competently she followed in his
wake, her flippered feet moving expertly, dark hair
streaming out behind her till he, turning unexpectedly,
caught her by it and brought her close to him. They
stared at each other for a few fraught seconds, then
surfaced and made their way back to the beach.

Leone was breathless by the time they reached the
shore and her fast-beating heart had little to do with
the exertions of the under water swim. And she could
see his chest rising and falling rapidly, she put out
her hand and touched the dark chest, hair sparkling
with crystal beads and his arms bound her closely to
him.

One quick pull of ribbon and the top of her bikini
was removed and his mouth was on her breast. Then
she was wrapped in one of the white fluffy towels, he
enveloped himself in another and they lay looking at
each other, the warmth and softness of the sand
adding to their feelings of contentment until they fell
asleep.

Preparing the meal that night Leone felt she was on
trial. In spite of what he had said she was still
smarting a little at his disparaging remarks about her
training, remarks which confirmed her own opinion of

what she had done in her life. So it was doubly important that she should prove that she had some talents.

The melon was easy and as it was in perfect condition she decided against any attempt to improve it. For the main course she intended to use the pork fillet she had found in the fridge, concocting a rather special sauce from dry cider and some calvados she found languishing in the store cupboard. It required just a hint of garlic and a teaspoonful of sugar to transform it into something special ... She replaced the lid on the skillet, turned her attention to a green salad, measured out the rice for cooking at the last minute and racked her brains over what to make for pudding.

It was much too late to think of anything that needed a great deal of time but she solved the problem with some peaches, sponge cakes and cream. With a discreet amount of brandy, some glacé cherries and nuts that would make a dessert fit for a celebration party.

Gray had already used the bathroom by the time she rushed down to the cabin and she took hardly any time at all to shower, preferring to use what time she had in repairing the ravages of too much time in the sun and sea. And too much happiness, she thought, with a stab of superstition lest it should disappear with the suddenness it had come.

The mauve dress was sensational she decided with rising excitement as she linked a narrow gold belt about her waist. Her hair was just a bit wild but on reflection she thought it suited her brilliant eyes and the hectic sunburn on her cheekbones. Tomorrow she must remember to use the filter cream she had specially bought, but at the moment the feverish look echoed her mood. Just a touch of lip gloss, a smear of molten gold on her eyelids and she was right.

Throughout the meal, which they ate at a table set under an awning on deck, her heart was beating an irrational tattoo and each intercepted glance across the table appeared to confirm that her feelings were shared. Once or twice his hand touched hers on the cloth as if by accident but tonight their eye-contact, fraught as it was with promises, was the most exciting feature. He had opened a bottle of champagne, she had decided against asking if they were celebrating, such questions could be dangerous. He told her the meal was delicious, sounding so contrite that she giggled unexpectedly into her glass, spluttering the liquid over her dress.

'That's expensive stuff.' He remonstrated while he offered his handkerchief to mop up. 'Even if it is smuggled.' He had insisted that he brought it in by the case load undetected by the customs and she hadn't known whether or not to believe him.

'I'm sorry.' She had regained control on the surface at least. 'You sounded so guilty for a moment.'

'Guilty?' He smiled in sympathy, although it was clear he was uncertain of her meaning.

'Guilty about questioning me over my . . . wasted youth.'

'Oh, that.' He grimaced. 'Well, I did say I was sorry. And now that I've tasted your coooking I take back everything I said about it. People who can cook like that in difficult circumstances can't be all bad.'

'Thank you.' Under the sweep of her long lashes she flirted audaciously.

'But now,' it was a moment before he went on and by then he had caught hold of her hand, his fingers were stroking her wrist, her pulses were hammering, 'there's another question I'm burning to ask.'

Burning was the only word that registered, perhaps

because it seemed so appropriate for the occasion. 'And what is that?'

'I want to know how . . . you came to be engaged to Simon Darcy.'

CHAPTER SIX

SOMEWHERE away to her right, light flashed and ran along the surface of the water. She looked round, startled but with blank eyes returning almost immediately to his face.

'Don't worry, Leone,' his eyes were tender, his voice gentle and the fingers on her skin a caress, 'it's just wildfire, we get quite a lot of it when the weather's hot like this.' And he waited.

'Simon?' Her voice faltered, eyes stung and she looked away from him, to the fingers so casually linked on the pale blue cloth. 'You were asking how I came to be engaged to Simon.'

'Mmm.' Severing the link between them, he reached to one side for a cheroot, clenched it between his teeth and, all without taking his eyes from her face, he lit it. The flame from the match wavered for a moment, strengthened and threw shadows on his face before it was extinguished. 'I wonder why, feeling as you do, you agreed to his proposal.'

Fury gripped her for a moment, how dared he question her about her motives, about what had happened before they had met? What she knew about his outlook on marriage denied him any right to comment on hers. But her anger subsided quickly as it had arisen. For she recognised that she longed to tell him, to explain, to get it off her conscience.

'You see, we were at a wedding last Easter. I was bridesmaid, he was best man. Both the bride and bridegroom were our best friends. We used to go round in a foursome when it suited us, no strings, or so we kept assuring each other.' She smiled at him wanly, an unconscious plea for understanding. 'Then Anita rang me suddenly and said she and David were getting married. I didn't believe her at first but she convinced me she had suddenly found she couldn't live without him. David was a widower and had a young son so I suppose it was all quite suitable. Anyway, now Anita's expecting a baby soon so it will complete their family.'

'But you and Simon . . .' he prompted.

'Well, it was all a bit heady, exciting. And when David and Anita left on their honeymoon, things maybe got out of hand, champagne was flowing like water and when Simon proposed, I just thought it would work.'

'And when,' he was now studying the glowing end of his cigar, 'did you . . . change your mind?'

'I . . .' A vision of Simon lying still and white on the hospital bed flicked into her mind and suddenly she knew she couldn't tell Gray the entire truth. Not till she had formally broken off her engagement with Simon. It would be so mean to Simon. Besides . . . Gray, with his antagonism to marriage, shouldn't expect to hear every last detail of what was none of his business . . . after all, she had no intention of quizzing him about Laverne. 'I haven't,' by some great effort she managed to inject some lightness into her voice, 'actually said I have changed my mind. It was *you* who told me I had.'

'Are you saying now that you haven't changed your mind? I did notice,' he raised her left hand to his lips, dark eyes surveying her with a careful, watchful look, his mouth touched the narrow silver band she had worn on her little finger since she was sixteen, 'when I picked you up in the hospital that you weren't wearing your engagement ring.'

'No, of course not.' She tried to maintain her lightness. 'It is an expensive ring and I don't wear it when I have my hands in and out of water as I do when I'm in the shop. How would I feel if I left it on the side of the sink?'

'Guilty, I should think.'

'Right. And it's not a feeling I enjoy.'

'So,' her remark had given him the opening he had been seeking, 'what about this? Us?'

'I'll just have to cope with that, won't I?'

'And are you sure that's what you want to do?'

'Look . . .' Suddenly, unable to bear any more she jumped up from the table. 'We're enjoying ourselves aren't we? I don't want to worry about Simon till I get back home. And I don't want to think about *anything*. Particularly now.' She bit back some tears. 'Okay?'

'Okay.' He rose, stood staring at her for a second in a silence she could have sworn was disturbed by a sigh but then, his arms came out and caught her, pulling her close enough to hear the agitated beating of her heart. Helpless she lay against him, hypnotised by that dark glittering stare till another sudden flare of light ran over the surface of the water. 'Don't be frightened.' The warmth and comfort of him prevented any such thought. 'It's just wildfire. It can't hurt you. I won't let it.'

Oh can't it? There was a second's clarity and despair before his mouth came down to claim hers. Oh, won't you? Then the teasing tongues of wildfire began to lick through her veins, quenching every doubt, wiping out all her fears.

For two days the *Sea Trekker* lay on the tide, drifting back and forth on a sea as kind and gentle as summer itself. By day they swam, clambered along the rocks looking for shrimps and sea urchins, lazed in sheltered corners reading, eating the picnics they had prepared for their days ashore, chatting idly but taking care to avoid matters that could be abrasive. She was taken aback when on the second day he mentioned quite casually that he had a sister living in Johannesburg.

'Your sister?' She paused in the act of taking a bite from a ripe peach, looked at him over the top of her paperback book. 'I didn't know you had a sister.'

'I would have thought,' he paused and watching him she saw the expression in his eyes, knew he was veering away from the obvious, 'I might have mentioned her.'

'No.' And neither did Simon, she told him silently. 'No, I thought you were an only child.'

'No, Carey is two years younger than I am. Her husband is an architect, a South African and she has two kids, boys, six and four.'

'So you stay with them when you're there?'

'Some of the time.'

'When did she leave the islands?'

'Oh, she's been away since she was twenty. She went through a bad spell but she's very happily married and things are just fine now.'

'And your parents . . .?' she prompted.

'Oh, I thought you would know that, too. My father was a missionary in what's now Zambia. No money in it of course but he loved the work. But my mother contracted black water fever when she went back after a break in Saint Helier and she died shortly afterwards. That was when I was nineteen. And Dad followed six months later. I think he just couldn't get along without her. They had never been apart you see. I don't suppose he realised until he was on his own. Anyway, the mission doctor put heart disease on the death certificate but he told me when I got out there that privately he thought the old man had died of a broken heart. *There's* something,' his grin was painful to see and she looked quickly down at her folded hands, 'for you to think about in these liberated days.'

'I . . . I think maybe there is such a thing.' She spoke softly and her hand went out to touch his comfortingly. The words echoed round her brain and hearing them a second time she wondered at herself. Broken hearts. Who was she kidding? Then realisation struck her like a blow. Wasn't that just what she herself was courting? If something didn't come out of this present situation, if he just got on to his boat and sailed away, did she really think she could cope. Was she trying to pretend to herself that she wouldn't be broken-hearted? The very idea was enough to make her numb with despair. And yet, she wouldn't exchange these few days. And nights . . .

Their nights were spent in making love and each time it seemed to grow more perfect, more passionate, more tender according to their mood but always more loving. Leone, unused to all the troughs and crests of intense emotions, marvelled. To think, she wondered as she lay in the pale moonlight of the cabin and looked at the dark figure spread out on the sheet beside her, to think she hadn't believed such feelings as this existed. Her body *ached* with love for him. She placed a hand beneath her breast, seeking the source of the ache.

'Leone.' He murmured her name, a hand came out towards her, eyes opened slightly and closed again. 'Darling, I . . .'

'Gray.' It was the most frustrating thing. 'Wh . . . what did you say, darling?' She touched his shoulder, then, unable to resist the sensation, spread out her fingers over his chest.

'Witch.' He said sleepily, pulling her closer to him. She felt her heart begin to pound again as his eyes opened fully, his hand was forceful against the back of her head, his mouth was warm, insistent on hers.

'So,' they arrived back at the farmhouse in the mid-morning and he dumped all her things in her bedroom, 'will you be able to occupy yourself till about six?' He caught her to him. 'Then if you insist, I'm prepared to take you back home to your parents. And Simon.' His eyes were darkly watchful and she had the longing to throw her arms round his neck and say she had no wish to be taken back to Simon. Ever. 'But if I can persuade you to wait another night . . .'

'Well . . .' Her sparkling glance told him she might be persuadable. 'I might just give Mother a ring . . .'

'I don't want to leave you but you know I have some business I must attend to . . .'

'Of course.' Lightly touching his lips she allowed him to go. 'And don't worry, I'll be perfectly all right. I want to wash my hair and give myself a facial.' She rubbed her face, assumed a critical expression. 'My skin looks like an old boot.'

His mouth curved into a smile. 'You know you don't think that for a second but I don't mind thinking of you spending the day with your pots and potions. So long as it's all for me. It'll cheer me up when I'm listening to some boring financial statistics.'

'Your Aunt Meg.' Her words reached him as he turned to the door. 'Will she be over?'

'What is today?' He frowned and then grinned. 'You see, you've made me forget the very days of the week. What is it? Friday. Well, this is the day she does all the shopping and she probably won't come till five so you'll see her then. No, you'll have the house to yourself. Except for Jeanette, that is. I think this is the day she does some baking so she's here most of the time. Goodbye, my sweet.' He stopped at the door, his hand on the knob.

'Goodbye.' She felt like weeping. It was the first time they had been separated since . . .

'And, Leone?'

'Yes,' she said eagerly.

'You are beautiful.' His face was solemn. 'You don't need any potions.'

She stood for a long time without moving, imagined she heard the distant sound of the car moving away. Her mouth curved upwards and then before she realised what she was doing, she was lying on the bed, weeping into the pillow. But they were tears of happiness, so intense that she thought her chest would burst.

It was a lovely lazy morning, she sat by the open window of the bedroom, idly brushing her hair, enjoying the feel of the warm drying air as it gently subsided. Until then she had not realised her room was directly above the kitchen but the sounds of pots and pans rattling were unmistakable. Only she was too comfortably content to let the noise disturb her and gradually she found herself giving in to the irresistible inclination to close her eyes.

She didn't sleep, just lingered pleasantly in the half-world between sleep and wakefulness and couldn't at first think what it was that had brought her so rudely back to earth, her pulses clamouring wildly. Then she smiled to herself as Jeanette's voice drifted upwards, relaxing into her chair again. It was obvious she had a friend visiting, that was all, they were having a gossip and, judging from the rattle of crockery, a cup of tea while they sat on the paving outside the kitchen door.

It was then that the second voice became more distinct, it was a voice she knew, which she had no difficulty in understanding, especially when accom-

panied by that irritating little laugh which she had
noticed before.

'And what about the boss, Jeanette? Are he and
she . . .?' The voice was slow and suggestive, making it
easy to imagine the knowing look in Laverne's green
eyes.

'Oh, Laverne.' Jeanette giggled in an excited,
shocked kind of way which she was thoroughly
enjoying. 'I don't know.'

'Well, you have your own opinions, haven't you?
They *have* been away on the yacht for a few nights,
isn't it so? And Lars was told his services would not be
required.'

'Oh, but Lars. He doesn't always go with Mr Gray,
does he?'

'Not when he's entertaining one of his lady friends
but . . .'

Making an effort Leone rose from her seat, walked
to the far side of the room where she leaned against
the wall. For a few moments she felt sick but couldn't
quite summon the determination to go across and slam
down the window. A screech from Jeanette cut
through her head like a knife but her shocked 'Oh,
Laverne . . .' pulled Leone like the most powerful
magnet back to her listening post beside the heavy silk
curtains.

'Ah yes, but that's because he told me all about it.'
Laverne made no attempt to conceal the spite in her
voice nor the impatience with which the other girl's
shushing admonitions were brushed aside. 'Nonsense,
she won't hear.' But she lowered her voice for a
moment so that strain as Leone might she missed a
few words.

'. . . think he was a bit unfair. After all, just because
he doesn't believe in marriage doesn't mean he should
try to save the whole of mankind. Some men actually

want to be married, poor idiots. But anyway, it was while we were coming back from South Africa, we were chatting and he told us he had this plan for preventing the marriage. He would make the bride fall in love with him, "Seduce the Bride" he began to call it, almost as if it was a board game like Monopoly or Scrabble. Oh it was all a bit of a joke and I didn't believe for a minute that he was serious but I think that beneath all that charm,' she spoke as if she had a great deal of personal experience of that potent force, 'he can be a bit of a swine. Well, we know he can. Men just don't make fortunes as quickly as he did without being prepared to trample people underfood. Sometimes I feel glad I'm not the least bit interested in money,' she said enviously.

'That's what puzzles me . . .'

'What's that, honey?' Laverne asked indulgently, patronisingly.

'People like you.' Jeanette went on innocently. 'People with no money. You don't have to work, yet you travel the world and don't seem to want for anything. How do you *do* it without money?'

'Hey.' Laverne was still indulgent but faintly reproving. 'What do you think I was doing on the *Trekker* on that journey from South Africa? It wasn't just a pleasure trip, you know. I *was* doing the cooking. Among other things of course.' She laughed suggestively.

'Oh yes, and I know what those other things would be.' The sound of chair legs scraping on paving signalled the end of the conversation. 'Ah well, it's all right for some but I have to work in the meantime. Give me your cup, Laverne, I'd best get busy with my baking. You waiting for some lunch? I'll be making some soon.'

'No, I don't think so but thanks, Jeanette. I was

just trying out this scooter and thought I'd pop out and see you. I told Lars I'd meet him at two and pick up something to eat in town. I'll be on my way.'

Leone stood by the open window listening to the diminishing sounds of voices without any interest in what was being said. She had heard enough. More than that. And now all she was aware of was the knot of hard pain, like a stone in the middle of her chest and was without any clear understanding of just what had caused it. For there was a chilling numbness in her brain which could have been protective had it continued.

But gradually the deadening paralysis left her, she moved forward to the centre of the room, her eyes falling on the large plastic shopping bag which held all the things she had brought from the yacht and from which her original navy blue dress was falling on to the bedcover. In an instant she knew what she was going to do and went into a vortex of wild activity which kept her mind from the pain she was suffering.

Ten minutes later she was ready. She surveyed her reflection, only half-recognising what she saw there. Her face was pale as death beneath the tan but she was too drained to want to do anything about it. The dress, she smoothed a hand over the fine material, silently blessing the advent of minicare fabrics, it wasn't too bad, just a little crumpled but not enough to be unwearable. Her hair she had pinned back firmly in a French pleat, it was almost dry and it gave her pleasure to remember that Gray liked her to wear it loose. More from habit than from any interest she smeared her mouth with a little colour, not even noticing that she did it badly so her lips had a lop-sided look.

A quick glance round the room, the last of her purchases were bundled into the plastic bag with everything else and she left the room without even a backward glance.

'A taxi, Miss?' Jeanette summoned from the kitchen stared at her. 'But I was just about to call you for some lunch.'

'Oh, I'm sorry, Jeanette.' Was that really her own voice, so calm and undisturbed? 'There must have been a misunderstanding. I'm going back home, I thought Mr Ellison would have told you.'

'No, he said . . .'

'Can you remember the number, Jeanette? For the taxi I mean.'

'Oh yes. I'll call it for you. At once, did you say?'

'If you would, Jeanette.'

While she was waiting for the car to arrive Leone disposed of the clothes by the simple means of handing them over to Jeanette.

'I shan't have any use for them now.' She smiled. 'They'll want washing but maybe you'll be able to find a home for them. Mr Ellison told me you have two sisters so . . .'

'Oh, Miss . . .' Clearly Jeanette was delighted. 'All these things. And moisturising cream and perfume.'

'Yes, I really can't be bothered taking them with me so if they're any good . . .'

'Oh, thank you. But . . . You're sure you won't have anything to eat?' Clearly the girl was still worried, 'I'm sure Mr Gray said . . .'

'I tell you what, I'll just write a little note for him in case he had the wrong end of the stick. Would that be better?'

'That would be best. And you'll find paper and envelopes in the cloakroom, the drawer just below the telephone.'

She didn't even know what she was going to write but in the end felt the words could not have been improved if she had considered them for a week.

Something inside her, pride probably, insisted that he should be denied the satisfaction of knowing how hurt and abused she felt. If that *had* been his plan then he would never know he had succeeded.

Dear Gray,

Just a line to say thank you. You have helped me such a lot. Now I think it's best for both of us to get back to normal and so I've decided to take the first boat back home. It would only complicate things if we became more involved and neither of us wants that. Love,

Leone

She re-read it, a bitter, cynical little smile twisting her lips. Then she had an inspiration and quickly dashed off a postscript.

I really enjoyed myself, hope you did too.

In the car driving into Saint Helier the casual wording of the letter gave her a great deal of satisfaction. She blessed the self-control which had stopped her telling him exactly how contemptible she thought he was, she suspected if she had given in to her inclination to explain how much of a swine she considered him, she would be feeling even worse than she was now.

She was sea-sick all the way back to the mainland. Divine justice, she supposed, the wages of sin although what she had done to deserve the same treatment on the way over she just couldn't think. Oh, yes, she could. She leaned her head wearily against the wash hand basin in the small cabin she had managed to book, that was a punishment for her treatment of Simon. Poor Simon!! The tears came easily. All that suffering just because she had changed her mind about marrying him. She lay down wearily on the bunk turned her head to the wall and wished she could just quietly die.

'Miss Leone!' Linda gaped at her as, having opened the front door with her key, Leone stepped into the hall. 'We didn't expect you back just yet. Lady Chevenix said . . .'

'Oh, where is my mother, Linda?' Best get that over before she did anything else.

'Your mother . . .? But I thought you knew . . .'

'Knew? Knew what?' With difficulty Leone hung on to her patience. It wasn't often Linda was as stupid as this.

'Sir Piers and Lady Chevenix have gone away for a few days. Up north. Cumberland I think she said. I've got her phone number somewhere . . .'

'Oh yes. I forgot.' Leone bit her lip. She had not realised her parents had intended leaving so soon. 'Oh well, I'll just go upstairs, Linda.' She ought to have paid more attention to her mother's plans.

'Are you . . .' the girl took a step closer, '. . . are you all right, Miss Leone? You're looking . . . very pale and washed out.'

'Oh, I'm fine, Linda.' Firmly she turned away and took a few steps towards the staircase. 'I just got off the ferry and I felt a bit sick coming over from Jersey. I didn't know I was such a bad sailor.'

'Oh, that'll be it then. I thought . . .' She bit off the words she had been about to speak, so Leone had little doubt she was thinking of the cancelled wedding, imagining she was still suffering the disappointment from that. If only they knew she thought bleakly, pulling herself up by the banisters as if she were an old woman, what on earth would they all think of . . .

'Would you like something to eat, Miss Leone? I could easily fix something on a tray.'

About to refuse Leone suddenly changed her mind

and turned to look down with a vestige of a smile. 'Oh, you know what I *would* like, Linda, if it's not too much trouble.'

'Of course. Anything.' Linda smiled her relief.

'A large pot of tea, I feel so thirsty and a slice of toast. When I've had that I think I'll just fall into bed and sleep the clock round.'

But in spite of her brave words she found that when she slipped, with a sigh of relief, into her own bed that all her yearning for oblivion was frustrated. Each time she closed her eyes, it seemed that Gray's image was etched there, he was coming closer to her, his voice murmuring her name and she actually found herself anticipating his kiss. In the end she found her only protection was to hold her eyes wide open, staring into the darkness. That had the double advantage of excluding him and preventing the tears which were just waiting to fall. Apart from that her heart ached as persistently as ever, she was even able to have a passionate mock debate on the subject of Gray Ellison, emerging at the end as bitter and wounded as ever.

At last, when the faint light of dawn was forcing itself between the chinks of her thick curtains she must have fallen into a light sleep but she woke around seven, unrefreshed and as unhappy as she had been when she got into bed the previous evening. There seemed little point in staying there so she rose and went downstairs where she went through a pretence of eating breakfast. But Linda was not taken in for she sighed as she cleared away the uneaten food and gave Leone a reproving look which could hardly be ignored.

'Sorry, Linda. But I promise by lunch time I'll be starving. It's just the after effects of the voyage and ... everything,' she said sadly.

'Of course.' Although she was little more than

eighteen, Linda was inclined to be motherly. 'It would be funny if you weren't like that, but you'll soon get back to normal again. I suppose you'll be going in to see Mr Darcy this afternoon.'

'Yes.' She had no idea how much of her weariness and reluctance showed through. 'Yes, of course I'll be going. But this morning, I think I'll go upstairs and do some jobs I ought to have done before. I'll do my own room, Linda, so you needn't worry . . .'

'All right, Miss Leone. Then I'll bring you up some coffee about eleven.'

But when she reached her room, Leone found that any idea she had had about tidying out cupboards and drawers was soon forgotten and she sat on a chair looking out of the window, no very coherent thoughts in her mind at all. It was such a mess. Getting engaged to Simon. She rose and brought out the ring he had given her, looked at it for a few moments before snapping shut the dark blue leather box. It was hard to think why . . . she couldn't imagine why she had ever thought she could marry him . . . But she had known so little about marriage then . . . She shivered, got up and found a pink cardigan which she draped around her shoulders. Now . . . She knew at least some of what it meant. The more intimate implications . . . And she knew with an absolute certainty that she could not contemplate marrying anyone . . . ever. In spite of what he had done, what she knew about him, she couldn't . . .

Coffee was brought about eleven and Leone forced herself to eat one of the biscuits arranged temptingly on a tiny plate. As well as being very proud of her baking, Mrs Godwin was a bit touchy and there was no point in offending her. She had just finished the coffee, was replacing her cup on the tray when sounds of a commotion, raised voices down in the hall forced her from her mood of almost total introspection. Without thinking what she was doing she pressed a hand to her middle as if trying to stem the tide of agitation. Then she checked herself for such stupidity, why should she imagine that every untoward happening should go back to him . . .

The disturbance had reached the very door of her bedroom and when it was thrown open, despite a protest from Linda, Leone retreated in panic to the farthest wall, arms crossed defensively over her chest.

'I'm . . . I'm sorry, Miss Leone. I tried to stop him but . . .'

Staring into the savage dark face which glared across the room at her, Leone only just managed to control her shudder. She took a step forward and abandoned her dramatic pose, when she spoke she was surprised at the sound of her calmness. 'It's all right, Linda.'

'But I . . .'

'As your mistress said, Linda,' his voice, too, confounded all he was so obviously feeling, 'it's all right.' All the blackness was wiped from his face as he smiled at the girl, his potent charm operating at full power. 'I'm sorry I was a bit impetuous downstairs. You see, Miss Chevenix and I have something rather important to discuss.'

Leone watched cynically while the girl softened in the influence of his deliberate manipulation, yet who could blame her? Dressed even as he was now, obviously straight from the yacht, navy slacks, white shirt and navy guernsey all adding to the study in potent masculinity, he would have been hard for any young girl to resist and Linda didn't even try. Broad shoulders, dark skin, sudden overwhelmingly charming smile and she gave way completely, her response so total that Leone felt an even more

ferocious twist of pain. She longed to rush towards
him, to thrust the girl away with an impatient little
gesture and to slip a possessive hand through his arm.
Jealousy. It couldn't be. She wasn't.

'It's quite all right, Linda. Really.' It felt such a
stupid smile she fixed on her face but it appeared to
deceive the girl who turned to the door. 'But maybe
Mr Ellison would like some coffee.' The girl paused to
look at him questioningly.

'No, thank you.' He glared at Leone but held the
door politely for Linda, closed it firmly when she had
gone.

And now she was alone with him Leone felt all her
frail self-assurance ebb swiftly. From now on her
whole strategy was bluff. She took a step forward,
sank down on to a stool and waved him casually to a
chair.

'Won't you sit down for a minute.' No use
encouraging him to think he was here for a
prolonged visit. 'I really didn't expect to see you
this . . .'

He ignored the invitation, advancing towards her in
a way that was distinctly chilling, stopping just a few
yards from her, close enough for her to interpret the
angry sparkle in his dark eyes.

'What the hell do you mean by baling out the way
you did?'

'I thought,' Laverne's amused words came back to
wound her, 'it was best to quit when I was winning.'
She smiled dazzlingly, it hurt her face. 'When we were
both winning. Isn't that what always happens in the
most satisfying of affairs?' Feeling quite pleased with
that she turned away from him but before she had
gone far she felt her arm caught in a ferocious grip
which wrenched her to her feet. Startled eyes flicked
upwards in a panic which must have betrayed her

feelings, she fought for control.

'And what would you know about it?' he spat.

A wave of colour swept into her cheeks then away from them, leaving her white and giddy. 'I know,' she tried to laugh, 'I know I haven't much experience of the situation but I've always heard . . .'

'So,' as suddenly as he had grabbed her, he pushed her away, as if she offended him, 'you're setting yourself up as a woman who's an expert on affairs. There's a name for women like that.'

'You should know.' Angry now and uncaring she threw the words at him, glaring furiously for a second before she remembered how she had intended to deal with him. 'But no, I hadn't had that in mind. Setting myself up as an expert on . . . what you said.'

'Don't be afraid of the word,' he jeered but she took a deep breath and ignored him.

'Once you told me,' the words had burned themselves into her mind so they were easily enough retrieved now, 'that it was time I had a little experience. You said that on the very first time we went out together, so don't blame me for taking your advice.'

'I was making a comment.' He spoke through his teeth and looked as if he would have liked to strangle her. 'Not giving advice, as I remember it.'

She laughed, and if the sound was a tone shriller than usual then she was certain he didn't notice. 'Oh, don't be so modest, Gray. You gave me advice and surely you won't be angry if I tell you I'm glad you did. It was good advice and I took it and I have no regrets.' She stumbled over the word, so ineptly chosen but there was no sign on his face that he had any recollection of having heard it before. 'None whatsoever.'

He did not speak but stood there, looking at her but

she knew from the rapid rise and fall of his chest that he was angry. Angry, she supposed, as much at having his deep laid plan subverted as having lost his temporary bedfellow. The word came into her mind and stayed there, she was remembering how warm and silky his skin felt against hers. She longed to run forward to him, to link her hands about his neck and beg him to make love to her. Just once more and it didn't matter if it meant his discovering just how successful his plan had been.

'In fact,' to save herself from committing the ultimate folly she hurried on, 'you were right on a number of accounts. You told me I was a victim of sexual frustration and you know, without me saying, just how right you were on that. I really,' unable to face him when she was uttering such humiliating and embarrassing lies she swung round in her chair, toyed with an ornament on the dressing-table, 'am most indebted to you. I truly appreciate all you did to help me.'

'It was a pleasure.' There was a sneer in his voice that could hardly be ignored but she pretended not to notice.

'Well, you know what they say,' she spread out her hands, palm upwards to emphasise her sincerity, 'men even these days are so much more experienced but more and more are expecting their wives to show a little expertise. I should have hated to be a disappointment to . . .'

'You know,' he drawled as he interrupted her, then made her wait while he lit a cheroot, looked round unsuccessfully for an ashtray before replacing the spent match in the box and returning it to his pocket, 'you know when I got that letter you wrote . . . Incidentally,' one dark hand came down briefly over his eyes, a gesture of extreme weariness which touched her, in spite of her contempt, 'I was later than I had hoped, it was after seven when I got back to the house. The meeting was a tough one and I was worn out. Then I found the place empty except for my aunt, and she like a cat on hot bricks because she couldn't think what had happened to you. When I got that letter, I thought there must be some mistake, You see,' his eyes narrowed, scrutinised her face so closely she was sure they must penetrate her flimsy façade, 'I couldn't equate that hard little note you left with the woman who had slept in my arms, the one who moaned so convincingly when I made love to her.' He spoke with such deliberate, relentless cruelty that Leone felt her heart being crushed in her chest, she had to struggle to hold on to her senses otherwise she would have slipped away into a faint at his feet. 'The woman who would have made love all night long, who begged me ...' He bit the words off as if he were angry with himself for reviving memories of what was best forgotten. Leone stifled the little moan that almost forced itself between bloodless lips.

'I'm ... I'm sorry.' She tried to sound as if she meant it but not too much so. 'I was clumsy and I can see your feelings are hurt. They needn't be, you know. I'm trying to explain, I learned such a lot from you and all of it was wonderful. I'm surprised at myself for not realising just how much I was missing.' The darkening of his face told her how he disliked that. Almost as much as she did herself. How could she tell disgusting lies with such fluency, she hadn't known she had it in her. Besides, she must be more careful. There was no use overemphasising just how wonderful she had found it or he might get the wrong idea.

'Anyway,' she tried to give the impression their interview was reaching a natural conclusion, she forced herself to stand up, to smile in what could be taken for a friendly manner; friendly but detached, 'you were right in saying inexperienced people shouldn't marry. And I think I'll make a much better wife for Simon as a result of the days we spent on the . . .'

The words were broken off as he came towards her again and took her by the shoulders. 'Are you telling me,' he hissed the words, 'that after what's happened between us you're *still* going to marry Simon Darcy?'

'*Still?*' She echoed the word in his exact tone but with a tiny puzzled frown on her face. 'What do you mean still? There's never been any question . . . Except,' her face cleared as if a penny had suddenly dropped, 'except in your imagination, of course. 'I never said I wasn't going to marry Simon.' She laughed. 'It was you who said that.'

He laughed with her, then his amusement cleared abruptly. 'I almost feel sorry for him.' His tone did not give any indication of a long-term friendship with Simon. 'But there is one other matter which has been exercising me.' The dark eyes bored contemptuously into hers which were wide with dismay and fear. 'It has I suppose,' he drawled the words as he left her, went over to the door where he leaned against the upright, 'occurred to you that there might be some . . . results from our little experiment. Or are you so naïve that you imagine the divine fates which have guarded you all through your pampered spoiled existence will protect you for ever against the results of your own folly?'

For just a few seconds his meaning escaped Leone, then when it did penetrate into her shocked mind she felt waves of shame assault her. It was something that *had* concerned her in the dark lonely hours of the night. Oh, not those nights when she had slept with his arms about her, when they might have been hell—or heaven—bent on creating new life, not on those nights. But when she had lain wide-eyed in the bed just behind her, the fear had crept unbidden into her thoughts and had been rejected as too frightening to contemplate. Her voice was perfectly steady once the colour had fled from her cheeks although it was with difficulty she was hanging on to the shreds of control. She even managed a tiny laugh which she strove to inject with a shade of condescension.

'I shouldn't worry about that. I'm not a complete fool you know. And besides, the idea of becoming pregnant on honeymoon is not one that appeals to women these days and as you know, Simon and I should have been . . .'

'I hope you're right.' He had crossed the room without her being aware of his intention, caught her again by the shoulders and dragged her close to him. 'By God, I do. For I would never allow a child of mine to be brought up as a Darcy.'

'I . . . I told you,' she said weakly, hoping he would not notice the hands clenched so tightly at her sides. Even a touch as critical and hostile as this was enough to turn her legs to jelly, the rest of her to a hungry, yearning fever and almost as if he could see into her mind, his expression changed, softened, his mouth curved, misleading her so that momentarily she weakened, held up her throat as he trailed a finger seductively down its length.

'And to think,' his voice was as vibrant as when he had made love to her, 'all day yesterday when I was run off my feet, the only thing in my mind was whether I could persuade you to come with me to the Azores. To fly there, if the idea of sailing was too much. Of the hours we could have spent out there doing . . . doing just what pleased us best.' His fingers rested gently against her breast where he was sure to feel the exaggerated beat of her heart and his mouth descended, touching hers with the lightest, most fleeting of kisses. And then he had left her and was striding to the door.

'Remember me when you let Darcy make love to you. Remember how my fingers scorched your skin, remember how you responded. And if he asks any questions, then you have my permission to tell him just who gave you your first lessons.' His grin was shocking in its animosity in the second before the door closed on him for good.

CHAPTER SEVEN

'You know, love,' Anita's hands hovered over the coffee pot and she slid a glance at her friend from behind long lashes, 'you're looking a bit better now. I really,' the coffee cup was handed across the table, distracting Leone's apparently rapt attention from the street scene just beyond the finely pleated net at the window of the lounge of the Lytchett Arms, 'think . . .'

'What were you saying, Anita?' Her cheeks coloured guiltily. 'I'm sorry, I thought I caught sight of Susan Hastie but . . .'

'But it wasn't.' Anita raised her cup to her lips and sipped. 'I know because she's supposed to be in Bermuda at the moment.'

'Oh yes. I forgot. She did say that when we met her last week, didn't she? Lucky thing,' she added automatically.

'Yes, I was saying,' dark brown eyes surveyed Leone's face critically, 'you are listening this time aren't you? I don't want to have to begin again.'

'I'm listening.' She grinned in an attempt to throw aside the depression which was becoming something of a habit. It wasn't fair to meet Anita every week and then be a wet blanket. She had been one for the past two months and it was time she snapped out of it. For everyone's sake. 'Go on then.'

'I was going to say that you're beginning to look a bit better. You know,' now all Anita's attention was claimed by the swirling contents of her cup as she added a little sugar, 'your friends have been quite worried about you.'

'I know.' There was a moment or two of lip biting before she went on. 'And I am grateful for everything, Anita. I'm trying to pull myself together.' There was a sparkle of tears in her eyes as Anita looked up at her. 'Isn't that what everyone tells you you ought to do?' To her dismay she was forced to search for a handkerchief in her bag and to blow her nose vigorously.

'It isn't always the easiest thing to do.' Anita's hand came out and squeezed Leone's. 'But anyway, so long as you're on the mend. I thought it was time to worry when David told me you were looking ill and losing weight. You know he's always been one of your greatest admirers.'

'Bless him.' Leone had recovered from her inclination to tears and she raised her cup and began to drink. 'You can tell him I'm fine now.'

'You can imagine how galling it is,' Anita sat back and placed a hand on her stomach, 'to hear your husband making comments about some people losing weight when you're feeling just like a barrage balloon.'

'Oh well.' Not knowing a great deal about these things Leone had once or twice thought her friend's pregnancy looked a little more advanced than it actually was. 'So long as the doctors don't think you're putting on too much weight.'

'No,' Anita's manner was suddenly non-committal, 'they don't seem to think that.'

'Maybe it will be twins. I suppose that might account for it.'

'Well, thank you very much.' In spite of her tone Anita was smiling. 'Here I am, in the last stages of pregnancy, willing to give up my time in trying to cheer you up while all you can do is fill me with the direst of fears. Do you think I *want* to cope wuth two infants?'

'Oh, Anita. You know you could manage.. Besides, if you were to have twins you could afford to have some extra help in the house.'

'Well, luckily I know I'm not having twins. Just one, I'm glad to say. And I really want to look after my own children, not farm them out to a nanny. I think you'll feel just the same when it comes to your turn.'

'Which looks,' the amusement faded from Leone's face as she handed over her cup for refilling, 'like being a long way ahead. If ever.' The bitterness slipped out before she could stop it.

'Oh, I don't know. These things happen when you're least expecting them.'

Leone did not trust herself to reply because she would have screamed, startling not only Anita but also all the mid-morning coffee crowd who usually gathered in the Lytchett on market days. 'I know,' she wanted to shout. 'I know how unexpectedly these things happen. No one knows it better than I do.' It was easy to imagine the shocked expressions that would focus in their direction, shocked that is until they realised just who was disturbing the unremarkable tranquillity of their lives. Then there would be exchanges of knowing looks, eyebrows would be raised and she would hear her name being passed from mouth to mouth. Her lips curved into a wry, almost cynical smile, one which misled her companion.

'Yes, they do, you know.' Anita raised a finger in the direction of the waitress and turned back to the table. 'After all, who would have thought a year ago . . .' There was a faint colour in her cheeks as she paid for the coffee then pushed back her chair, levering her clumsy figure upwards with a hand on the table. 'I must go to the loo,' she whispered, 'that's one of the penalties . . .'

While she waited in the powder room for Anita, Leone studied herself in the mirror, deciding at last that there was some truth in what she had been told. The expression of despair, of sheer misery which had haunted her features for so long had gone. Or at least, she made the mental correction, it was no longer on public display for she had finally passed the stage of not caring who knew the depths of her unhappiness.

That short spell in London with her cousin Mark had helped. No one thrown into his company for any length of time was given peace to brood, that was probably why her father had made the suggestion. And there had been shopping expeditions arranged for the times when Mark could not entertain her but with one of his several women friends to guide her to some of the lesser known boutiques. The short velvet jacket she was wearing today, its rich plum colour picked up by one of the shades in her kilted skirt, had been one of her purchases and ...

'Didn't I tell you,' Anita's head appeared behind her in the glass, 'you *are* looking like your own self, whereas I,' she looked dismayed, 'defy description.'

'No, you don't.' Quickly Leone smeared some colour on to her lips. 'Besides, it must have been what you wanted or ...' She stopped wondering if she had gone too far. 'These days.' She smiled apologetically and shrugged.

'Oh yes, these days people have it all taped.' Now it was Anita's turn to fiddle with her make-up. Leone watched admiringly as she skilfully applied a little more colour to her cheeks, touched her lashes with a brown which enhanced her deeply set eyes. 'Except that some of us just act first and think afterwards.' Now her cheeks were crimson. 'Oh, Leone love, has it never crossed your mind that my marriage to David was just a little bit on the sudden side?'

Leone stared, for the moment unable to understand the trend of the conversation, yet admitting that yes, once or twice she had wondered. But such an unworthy idea had received the instant banishment it deserved. She gazed at her friend, trying to come to terms with the implications of what was being suggested.

'Oh, I'm sorry, Leone. This isn't the time but I've wanted to tell you for just ages. I've felt so guilty. And then your broken engagement, it seemed you had enough on your mind without worrying about me.'

'Worrying? I don't think I would have worried. Not unless it had been very obvious that you were unhappy.' She looked up as the door opened and a couple of elderly women came in. 'Shall we go then?' she enquired cheerfully and nothing further was said till they were outside in the car park. 'And you aren't are you, Anita?' As they reached the grey Jaguar she took her friend by the arm and turned her round. 'Unhappy, I mean.'

'No,' Anita shook her head so her brown curls danced round her face, 'I'm as happy as anyone *can* be. Probably happier than I *ought* to be. Come on and sit in the car.' Swiftly she unlocked the door and slid into the driver's seat, unlatching the passenger door for Leone. 'I want to tell you the whole story now, to get it off my chest at last.' She grinned mischievously. 'You're sure I'm not going to shock your Puritan morals?'

'I think they might be able to stand it.'

'Well then, you remember all that nonsense about me not being interested in David?'

'I didn't realise it was nonsense.' She pretended to be prim.

'Well, that was the idea. I didn't mean anyone to know but I had always fancied him. More than that, I had been in love with him for more than a year I suppose. Only, I knew how he felt about Danielle and didn't imagine he'd ever want to remarry. At least not for years and years. Then one night when we had been out, just after my birthday it was, I asked him up to have a cup of coffee.' Anita appeared to be absorbed in a tiny piece of thread that was hanging from the cuff of her glove. 'That was when it happened. Oh, I know I ought to feel ashamed, but I don't. I was prepared to settle for that. Then, next day he came round, to see if I was . . . all right. You know what I mean, but of course I had no idea. If it had been planned then I would have made sure, but it wasn't. Anyway, it was then he asked me to marry him. At first I thought it must be because he was worried about the possibility of my being pregnant but then gradually it came out that he had been feeling much the same as I had been. He had been afraid that I wouldn't like the idea of bringing up someone else's son so in the end it was the best thing that could have happened. We started planning the wedding at once and by the time we were married I knew positively I was pregnant. That was why I wore a pink dress instead of white but anyway I don't suit white so that didn't matter. Still, I keep hoping that she,' a loving hand was laid on the bulge, 'will be just a week or two late in arriving and not cause too much of a scandal in the neighbourhood and at Dame Agnes's in particular.' Until her marriage, Anita had been teaching English at Dame Agnes Latymer's School for Girls on the outskirts of the town.

'If it's a she, as you seem convinced, then you'll be able to put her name down for a place in eleven years, that should turn away any wrath they might be feeling.'

'I did think of that,' Anita grinned, 'but of course, if it's a boy he'll have to join Davey at Pendlebury.'

'Pendlebury?' Leone's head jerked round to look at

Anita. 'I didn't know Davey would be going there.'

'But of course.' Anita opened her eyes wide, emphasising her words with a little bit of mockery. 'The local grammar school isn't good enough for the Sheddens, they must go to Pendlebury. If they are boys, that is.' She yawned slightly. 'Like father like son, I suppose.'

'Do you mean . . . David went to Pendlebury?'

'Yes, didn't you know?' Anita inserted a key into the ignition. 'I thought everybody knew that. He and Simon used to speak about it often enough. Though I think David was just a year or two senior. Well, I must go, love. Davey will be home for lunch and he likes me to be there. It's great how he's accepted me, comes in yelling Mum, Mum. I suppose that's because he can't remember his own mother.'

'Well, I enjoyed the coffee.' Leone put her fingers on the door handle. 'Same time next week. Shedden minor permitting of course.'

It was a second before the slight joke was appreciated and then Anita let out a groan of protest. 'Don't say that, she might hear and think I'm impatient. No, you mustn't come early, whatever you do. David has too many maiden aunts sitting waiting, half-expecting to be shocked.'

'Don't worry.' Leone laughed. 'But thank you for telling me, love. I never guessed, not for a second.' It wasn't absolutely true, but near enough. 'Take care.'

'Thanks, Leone. I feel a whole lot better since I told you. See you next week as you said. And you must come out for dinner one night before I get my hands filled. I'll try and fix up a night with David and let you know. Oh and, Leone,' she had switched on the engine but her words stopped her friend slamming the door, 'I forgot to ask about Ma Darcy.' This was her habitual way of referring to Simon's mother. 'Any sign of her coming round yet?'

'Not really.' Leone shrugged, unable just yet to confide some news she had heard the previous day. 'She did pop in yesterday to see Mother but ... she made no attempt to hide her feelings for me.'

'I shouldn't worry.' Anita engaged gear. 'That's one trouble you have avoided for I swear she would have been a terrible mother-in-law. You'd have found she'd have wanted almost to *live* in your house, she's *so* possessive about her son.'

And that was true, thought Leone as she, rather more slowly than Anita had done, drove out of the car park and through the town. But instead of going directly home she found herself on the road which had become so familiar over the past weeks, driving in the direction of the cove where Gray had taken her. Anita's words still rankled, aroused all the guilty feelings she was trying to sweep aside.

For it was her fault that a lifetime's friendship between her mother and Simon's had been damaged beyond repair by her actions. She shivered a little as she turned into the narrow lane leading down to the tiny cove, pulled on the hand brake and got out of the car, at the same time fumbling in her handbag for a cigarette, a new habit but one which she had come to value, especially when she was feeling particularly fraught. Like now. Her fingers shook as she extinguished the match and returned it to the box, then she allowed herself to sink down on to the sand, in much the same spot where they had lain together.

But now the soft warm air of summer had given way to cooler days. Today there was a strong sharp wind coming from the sea, tangling her hair as it blew back from her face. She watched the waves racing in, breaking in swirling foam on the shore a hundred yards in front of her. How impossible it would be to sail on seas like these, in that little boat. She shivered in anxiety for his safety then with firmness forced her mind away from matters which didn't concern her.

Now Mrs Darcy did. She puffed at the cigarette, drawing the comforting smoke deep into her lungs, exhaling slowly. And she would never be quite free of the guilt for her broken engagement, even if, in the end, it had been much easier than she could have dared to hope. In fact, an excuse was handed to her on a plate if she had chosen to use it. But she was too honest to try to shift the blame from herself, even when it would have been so easy to do.

Her heart had been hammering against the wall of her chest as she made her way up to the hospital on the afternoon of the day she had the final scene with Gray. She was in such a state that had her parents been at home she would have asked her father to drive her but as they weren't she made the trip on her own.

On her way along the corridor she met someone who stopped her with a friendly query about Simon, a query which she answered but she could never afterwards identify the person, presumably a friend, who asked the question. In fact she was in such a state of inner tensions that when she reached the door of Simon's room, she didn't even think of knocking before she pushed open the door and stepped inside.

For at least ten seconds she stood there, convinced that she was seeing things that weren't happening, that her eyes were conveying pictures that belonged elsewhere, to another person. For what possible sense could there be in Janet Maine lying over the patient, feet quite off the floor she noticed blankly and with Simon's hands spread out over the fairly ample back of her navy uniform. That they were Simon's hands was incontestable, for there on the little finger of his right hand was the signet ring he had always worn.

There was a soft smacking sound which would have been hilarious in any *Carry On* farce but which didn't cause even the beginnings of a smile on Leone's uncomprehending face. She heard Simon give a faint groan, not the kind of indication of frustrated passion she was used to hearing from him but just then, before she could decide to go out, knock and wait for permission to enter, she felt the door swing against the small of her back and she looked up into the face of Mr Swithin, the senior orthopaedic consultant. He blinked down at her from behind his owlish glasses but before he could smile in his usual friendly way his gaze had moved to the couple on the bed, now showing urgent signs of even more intimate exchanges.

Then, rather mildly, Mr Swithin cleared his throat apologetically and at once Sister Maine, with great presence of mind, Leone thought dispassionately, began pulling at the pillows behind Simon's head and the face she turned towards the door, seconds later was surprisingly composed. True, there were two spots of high colour in her cheekbones and her dark eyes snapped angrily at Leone but on the whole she carried the embarrassment off well, even attacking Leone for coming into the room without permission.

'It isn't quite visiting time you know.' She glanced at the fob watch she wore on her bodice.

But Leone hardly heard the remonstration for she was looking at Simon, who was showing enough awkwardness for both of them, lying back in the narrow hospital bed and looking as if he wanted to be swallowed up by some natural disaster.

'Besides,' Janet Maine went on in her normal acidulated tones, 'Mr Darcy is seeing his consultant.'

'Oh, that can wait, Sister.' Clearly the situation was

one which even senior consultants fought shy of. 'You have your visit with your young . . . man, Leone, my dear.' He was a golfing friend of her father and she knew him quite well. 'I have several other patients to see and can come back here in about . . . an hour say.' With that he backed out of the doorway and his footsteps could be heard as he hurried down the corridor.

At last Leone found her voice and when she spoke she imagined her feelings were making themselves heard clearly enough. 'If you would be so kind, Sister. I would like to spend some time with my fiancé.' And her eyes must have gleamed menacingly for Sister Maine said nothing, but turned again to her patient.

'I'll be back as soon as possible, Simon,' she said reassuringly, 'to continue the treatment.' They were words that she must have regretted ever afterwards but they were spoken without thought and she whirled away before she could put her foot in it again.

For a long time Leone stood without moving and then slowly she went closer to the bed. There was no way she was going to break off her engagement at the top of her voice, especially with Sister Maine probably skulking about in the corridor in the hope of picking up any indiscreet words.

'Leone.' He didn't quite look into her eyes but held out a hand towards her. 'I . . . I didn't know you'd got back. How were the Channel Isles?'

'Simon. I'm sorry.' She didn't even realise she had ignored his question. 'I brought you this.' Afterwards she thought it had been a clumsy way to do it. Instead of the ring he must have been expecting some little memento of her holiday. But he put out a hand then stared down at the tiny box in baffled disbelief.

'Wh . . . what is this?' As he spoke he pressed the stud, blinked at the extravagant diamond. 'Leone, wh ... what do you mean. You can't ... you can't ...'

'I'm sorry, Simon. I'm not doing this very well ...'

'But, Leone,' his voice had a faintly whining, self-pitying note which grated against her nerves, 'you *can't*. Not just because of what ... what just happened. It meant nothing you know, I ...'

'Oh that.' Just then, for the first time she could see some connection. 'It was nothing to do with that.'

'Of course it was. And you're right to be angry, Leone. It was just a bit of fun, something that happened on the spur of the moment. You see, I had been lying here, half asleep and thinking of you. Wanting you, Leone. And then when I opened my eyes Janet was leaning over me straightening the pillow and I thought it was you.'

'Thank you.' Leone's sardonic remark surprised herself but Simon didn't even notice it.

He had raised himself on to his elbows and his face was scarlet with agitation. 'You *can't* break off our engagement, Leone. What will people think? What about my mother? And yours? They'll be stunned and heart-broken.'

'We weren't getting married just to please our parents, Simon.' Now that she had actually told him she was feeling much calmer, more in command of the situation and besides some of the weight had slipped from her shoulders. 'At least I hope we weren't. If that was the idea then we were fools ever to get into that position.'

'Leone. Please. If it hadn't been for my damned accident then we would have been married by now.'

'Well, I'm sorry about your accident, Simon, but maybe it was for the best ...'

'For the best?' His voice was shrill with indignation. 'If you had been the one who was nearly killed, I certainly shouldn't have suggested that was for the best.'

'No.' She felt ashamed of herself. 'No, I didn't mean that, Simon. But it gave us time to think.'

'You're just trying to punish me, Leone.' He said huffily. 'Just because of a silly little incident that meant nothing and . . .'

'It had nothing to do with that. I've told you. It's *my* fault, Simon, I made a mistake that's all.'

'Oh, did you? Well, you certainly choose your moments to tell a chap that you're not going to marry him. I love you, Leone, does that mean nothing?'

'I'm not sure that you do love me, Simon. You just think you do. After all, what man would send his fiancée away with another man, force her to go out with him against her will.'

'I was trying to cheer you up, can't you see that. And your father said you needed to get away for a bit.'

'That didn't mean I ought to go with Gray Ellison, you . . .'

'Why not go with Gray? I could rely on him looking after you properly. Besides, he suggested it. When Janet was in the room . . .'

'Janet,' she spat the name at him, 'do you mean Janet Maine?'

'Yes.' He held wide his hands so she could see how clean they were. 'I think it was her idea, and I thought it a good one. I wanted you to get to know each other.'

'Well,' bitterness spilled out unhindered, 'I don't think it was such a good idea, Simon.'

'You don't mean . . .' His eyes narrowed as he looked at her. 'You can't mean that you and Gray . . .'

'Oh, Simon,' she couldn't bring herself to lie directly but then she would never regard him as a confessor either, 'you ought to have known that I couldn't stand the man. Every time you spoke of him I used to feel my hackles rise. I'm going now.' She put out a hand and touched the hands that were clenched on the covers. 'I hope you won't think too badly of me, Simon. Maybe in the long run we can be, not friends exactly but not deadly enemies either.' It was all so clichéd she thought.

'I don't think that's very likely, do you, Leone?'

'Well, maybe not. But it hasn't been easy to come and tell you this. But I hope that soon you'll find that you're just a bit relieved, too. Goodbye, Simon.' She looked at him for a moment and when he didn't reply she opened the door and went out, reaching the main entrance without looking either to right or to left although she knew that Janet Maine was hovering about at the door of the main ward when she left Simon's room. That's someone who will be pleased, she told herself bleakly as she drove home. But she was fairly certain that the sister would be the only one to find any pleasure in the broken engagement.

Her parents were shocked and stunned by the announcement but curiously not as shocked, not as stunned as she had expected them to be. At least, once they knew she was adamant their support was total, her mother being particularly defensive against the wildest of Meggy Darcy's attacks.

For of course, all hell had been let loose once Mrs Darcy discovered that her darling had been let down so badly.

'I don't think Simon deserved to be treated like this. Especially not in the tragic circumstances.'

'Of course he didn't *deserve* it.' Flanked by her parents Leone faced her accuser courageously. 'I didn't break off our engagement to pay him back for anything.' Into her mind a picture of Simon with Janet Maine forced itself but she pushed it away.

'How *could* you, Leone? After all he's been

through. And what will people *say*? What will they *think*?'

'Oh, does it matter?' Leone found herself suddenly weary. The strain showed in the dark shadows beneath her eyes, the haunted expression which made her look drawn and ill. 'If it will help then he can say *he* broke it off. I don't mind.' She shook her head distractedly, 'I really don't mind.'

'Why should *you* mind?' Mrs Darcy ignored the placating fingers her husband placed on her arm. 'Why should you mind? No one has treated you abominably. And,' the full import of what Leone had suggested dawned belatedly, 'why should Simon take the blame? Is that what you're suggesting, that he should be accused of letting you down? Never.' It was impossible for her to hide her vindictiveness. 'Over my dead body.'

'Oh, all right. I just thought. No one likes to be rejected, to be pitied.'

'You should have thought of that before then, shouldn't you, Leone?' Mrs Darcy was having difficulty in retaining any control. 'But I can't say I'm surprised,' a sob escaped her lips, 'I never really thought you were suited.'

'In that case,' Leone felt as if all the blood had drained from her face, 'maybe you ought to be relieved instead of angry.'

'Relieved?' Mrs Darcy gathered her strength for another onslaught. 'Relieved to think the whole town's gossiping about us, laughing that my son has been jilted?'

'Hush now, Meggy. You're getting too worked up. You know you were pleased about Simon and Leone and we're sorry,' his eyes, as John Darcy looked at the girl, were troubled, 'really sorry that it hasn't worked out. But, let's admit that it took a bit of courage to call things off. It can't have been easy.'

'Easy,' Mrs Darcy commented tearfully. 'If she had any consideration . . .'

'Come on now, Meggy.' Sir Piers was at his diplomatic best but clearly he was not going to have his daughter bullied. 'You've had your say and I think we all understand how you feel. It has been a knock for all of us but I think Leone has gone through enough.' He ignored the snort of disbelief which suggested only when she had been stretched on a rack would she have suffered enough. 'And you might be relieved to know that I'm inclined to agree with you.' He smiled encouragingly into Mrs Darcy's suspicious face. 'I wasn't all that convinced Leone and Simon were suited.'

'Well . . .' She began again explosively then allowed Sir Piers to continue without demanding to know what possible objection anyone could have to Simon as a son-in-law.

'Not of course that we weren't delighted when we heard the news but there was just something. I'm glad we can agree on that at least, my dear. Now, you know how much we value your friendship, you and John are our oldest friends in the neighbourhood and it would be so sad if, because of this, we were to drift apart.'

'Of course we're bound to.' Mrs Darcy sniffed and dabbed at her nose with a hankie. 'That's another thing, Leone. Your mother and I have been friends since we were at school together and because of you, all that is ruined. Just tossed away.'

And Leone, who felt she had had enough, determined that Mrs Darcy should not see her crying, just ran out of the room and upstairs to her bedroom. Although the fit of weeping did not last long she was still lying on her bed when her father came into the room half an hour later. She acknowledged his presence with an upward flick of lashes and when he sat down on the edge of the bed and put his hand on her shoulder, the tears threatened again.

'Don't worry, Leone. That's the worst over now. From now on things will be easier.'

'I hope so.' She managed to produce a watery smile. 'For I don't think I would like to go through another afternoon like that. Nor,' the enormity of what she had forced her parents to endure had become even more apparent over the last forty-eight hours, 'nor to put you and Mummy through it.'

'We'll survive.' He patted her reassuringly. 'Even Meggy Darcy was less frightening than the Mau-Mau.'

Unwillingly, Leone laughed.

'And, I want you to know I was proud of you down there. It was a horrible position for you to be in and you faced up to it bravely. Lots of girls would have run away but I'm glad you didn't.'

'Thanks, Dad.' She found his hand and squeezed it. 'You and Mum have been wonderful. I hope it doesn't spoil things for you. With the Darcys I mean.'

'Oh, don't let it worry you. I'm sure Meggy will come round. After all, she doesn't have so many friends she can afford to be too high-handed.'

'Still, it's pretty awful for her, too. Especially as she's so fixed on her only son.'

'You know what I think, I think maybe she's rather pleased, she may not even realise it herself yet, but I think she would prefer it if Simon didn't marry at all.'

'From what she says she was never all that keen on me as a daughter-in-law. I suppose if I hadn't been your daughter she might have nipped things in the bud before now.'

'Mmm. Well, I don't know. I don't think Simon is so much under her thumb but . . .'

'Oh, and you. Did you say you had your doubts, too?' She giggled although she hadn't the least sense of amusement. 'If you could have seen her face.'

'But I did.' He smiled. 'Yes, she did seem to have the wind taken out of her sails, didn't she? But no, I was perfectly serious, I *did* have a question mark in my mind about you and Simon. It was just a bit too sudden . . .'

'Don't you believe then that people can fall in love almost at once?' A dark face hovered in front of her eyes for a second but when her father spoke again the disturbing image vanished.

'Of course I do.' As he smoothed back the damp hair from her forehead he smiled. 'That's how all the best love affairs begin. But I can't see it starting suddenly between a young couple who've known each other for most of their lives and who have never shown the faintest signs of being involved. Oh, at first I was pleased when you got engaged but then, things began to come back. And I began to wonder if I wanted Simon for a son-in-law.'

'Oh, I didn't know you disliked him.'

'I don't. Only I've always hoped that you would marry someone I could take to enthusiastically. And Simon is just a little bit bland for my taste.'

'Oh, Daddy.' As she squeezed his hand she suddenly yawned.

'Now,' he got up from the bed and pulled an eiderdown over her. 'I'm going to insist you have a sleep. It's my guess you won't have slept much for a night or two. And then tomorrow I'm going to run you up to town to stay with Mark for a week or two till all this blows over.'

'Oh, must I? He's so exhausting with all his concerts and shows.'

'Just what you need. It will take your mind off all

your worries and by the time you come back things here will have quietened down.'

They hadn't, of course. Each time she went into a shop in Heywood after her return from London she sensed the curious glances, imagined even if she couldn't quite see or hear, whispered messages from behind hands. But gradually she found she was minding less and less, although she still hadn't seen Simon face to face.

As Sir Piers had anticipated, Mrs Darcy had resumed her visits to Clarewood, perhaps not with the frequency of former times but she was not prepared to be excluded from the circle of the Chevenix family with all the social cachet implied by the title. Her encounters with Leone had been brief and frosty, at least on one side, and usually Leone tried to avoid her.

But she was sitting with her mother one afternoon when Mrs Darcy was announced and it would have seemed awkward to make her escape immediately, so she sat still, waiting for an appropriate moment to make her exit.

'And how,' Lady Chevenix had determined their conversations were to be as natural as possible and the enquiry was one she made regularly, 'is Simon? You said he would be getting back to the office this week?'

'Oh yes.' Mrs Darcy looked so flustered that Leone who had been meaning to look elsewhere found her attention riveted. 'Oh yes, he did go back but . . . He was still tired and shocked so the doctor ordered a complete holiday. Poor darling he . . .' She caught Leone's eyes and looked away. 'Anyway, he flew off to the West Indies yesterday. For a nice relaxing break in the sunshine.'

There was a longish silence which seemed to add to Mrs Darcy's confusion till Lady Chevenix spoke again. 'Really, Meggy. I am surprised. I had no idea he would be fit enough to make such a journey on his own. And to look after himself for ... how long did you say he was going to be away ...?'

'Oh, three weeks.' Mrs Darcy was very conscious of the colour in her cheeks but she faced them boldly. 'But I didn't say he was on his own, Enid. Of course not. The doctors would never have allowed it. No, of course not. He was allowed to make the journey on the strict understanding that he had efficient nursing help when he was over there. And just by chance, a fantastic piece of luck really, one of the nurses in the hospital agreed to accompany him.'

'Lucky old Simon.' Leone was uncertain whether the words had actually issued in a sarcastic drawl from her throat, afterwards her mother confirmed that they had not. But she was sure Mrs Darcy heard them for she drew in her breath in a disapproving hiss and looked daggers across the room.

'Yes, it's all worked out beautifully.' Now that he's not going to marry you, her eyes implied. 'And there's no one more dependable than Janet Maine.'

Leone, having sat too long on the sand got stiffly to her feet and went back to her car. She didn't begrudge Simon his few weeks of fun, or as much fun as he could have with part of his leg still enclosed in plaster. But still, having professional advice on the spot should resolve most difficulties. Miaow. She made a little face at herself as she backed out of the lane. Actually she rather hoped he would marry Janet Maine. If anyone could challenge Mrs Darcy then she was that one person. Now, she must get home because after lunch she meant to wash her hair and she had forgotten to buy the shampoo she preferred.

She was hurrying along the main street, pulling up the collar of her jacket and wishing she had brought a scarf to keep the wind from her ears when a hand came out and detained her.

'Miss Chevenix?'

'Yes.' For a second or two Leone stared, unable to equate the figure in front of her with the woman who had caused her such pangs of jealousy. Laverne O'Casey was a summer bird and now that winds were whipping the grey seas to cold peaks she seemed entirely out of her element, bleakly shivering, pulling the edges of her inadequate jacket together, then pushing a strand of hair under her less than jaunty yachting cap. Only then did Leone recognise her.

'Laverne. Miss O'Casey.' She corrected herself when the other woman grinned. Leone noticed that she looked older, all the tiny lines about her eyes were exaggerated and her features were pinched.

'Oh, Laverne's good enough. No one calls me Miss O'Casey.' Abruptly the smile faded. 'Have you heard?'

'Heard?' A feeling of dread, at once familiar and yet unknown seized Leone, a flashing recollection of the premonition she had had a short time ago back on the beach came to her. 'I don't understand . . .'

'The *Trekker* is overdue.' Laverne looked away from Leone, vaguely in the direction of the winding narrow street that led to the harbour. 'It should have returned to Heyport on Tuesday.'

'And . . . you haven't heard?' Her lips were stiff, her voice sounded faint and distant.

'Just a wireless message, to say they were making poor time in mountainous seas.' She shrugged and her smile was a travesty of the confident self-assurance of Laverne O'Casey. 'But I expect they'll be okay. Don't they say, the devil looks after his own.' She waved a casual hand. 'Well, I'll see you around maybe.' And she began to move on.

'Just a minute.' Impulsively Leone put her hand on the woman's arm. 'What about you? Where are you staying?'

'Oh, I'm all right. Didn't I say,' she grinned showing the white teeth which were less startling now that her tan had faded, 'the devil looks after his own? I got a job down in the Mariners' Arms. Part time, but it provides a roof over my head and besides,' she was suddenly serious again, 'it's a good situation for keeping an eye on the boats coming and going.' And with that she swung away, quite as if she were regretting whatever impulse had caused her to stop Leone.

It was a struggle for Leone to sit through the midday meal with her mother as if nothing had happened. Luckily Sir Piers was lunching at the golf club that day for she suspected that his much more perceptive eye would have suspected something was wrong. As it was, she was able to hide the tumult of anguish she was suffering, although it was impossible for her to banish from her mind the picture of a yacht battered by savage waters, she saw, with hideous clarity the saloon awash, the boat gradually losing the battle, overwhelmed and then sinking. Hands struggling for a long time, clinging to bits of debris before they, too, gave up the unequal contest.

'I think, Mother,' as soon as she could she pushed back the chair, 'I'll go up and have a lie down. I've got a bit of a headache.' And her mother, with the solicitude she had shown since the breaking of the engagement, allowed her to leave without comment.

She was unable to cry and that was the most painful experience of all. If she had been able to weep she would have got relief from the horrible, stupid impression of a large stone lodged in the area of her chest. And yet she couldn't. And it was impossible for her even to sleep.

At last she could stand it no longer. She got up from her bed, pulled on a pair of navy, checked trousers and

topped them with a warm reefer jacket. She didn't
notice how elegant she looked but bundled her long
hair inside a knitted cap, aware only of a deep-set chill
and the need to wrap up warmly.

Before she understood her motives or intentions she
was parking her car in a corner of the harbour area and
huddled against the wind was walking along the
quayside. She shivered as her eyes caught sight of the
huge waves battering against the boom which
protected the entrance to the basin, her imagination
caught up again in the horror of her thoughts.

There was no sign of the *Sea Trekker*, it took her
only a few minutes to walk alongside to ascertain that
fact and, with a barely suppressed sob, she turned and
hurried back to her car. For a long time she sat there,
staring through the spatter of rain on the windscreen,
her mind almost completely blank but for the pressure
of some awful unidentified grief.

It was growing dark when obeying another impulse
she threw herself out of the car again, hurrying back
down the steep cobbles, pushed on to the quayside by
an especially strong flurry of wind. Ahead of her, she
caught sight of a racing figure and the impetuous cry
that came to her lips was snatched away by a gust of
wind.

More slowly now and keeping to the shadowy
shelter of the buildings Leone followed Laverne
O'Casey's flying figure. And then, in the light spilling
out from some street lamps she saw the boat being tied
up, her heart was racing as she stood in the doorway,
eyes narrowed against the darkness and intermittent
spots of rain as she tried to make it out.

Her heart was beating in wild agitation against her
chest, her mouth was suddenly dry as she recognised
the tall shape, dressed in yellow oilskins and pulling a
navy cap from his head as he loped across the casually

tossed down gangway. Then she watched Gray seize
Laverne in his arms, the flash of white teeth as he
grinned was like a stab straight to her heart and
Leone withdrew still more deeply into the shadows.
Her feet stumbled as she found the flight of steps
leading to the shipchandlers' alley, her eyes blurred
with tears as hurriedly she made her way up the
steep street, through a little covered archway into a
courtyard and thence by a roundabout route to her
car.

It took her quite a few moments of painful struggle
to reach a stage when she felt it safe to drive her car
the distance back to Clarewood and even then she
hesitated, torn between anger and overwhelming
relief.

Relief should have been the only emotion, she
recognised that easily enough, but it was impossible
for her to deny the anger and jealousy that had ripped
through her as she watched their coming together on
the quayside. All she possessed in the world she would
have given to buy herself the right to greet him, the
right to be swept round in that arc of glorious
triumph, to feel the warm salty touch of his mouth on
hers. Though to be honest, she had chickened out of
watching this last, turning away in an effort to protect
herself from further lacerations.

She shivered again, reached out and switched on the
ignition and as she drove home she endeavoured to
come to terms with what she had just seen. The
alternative which had tormented her for several hours
was now unbearable to contemplate and she must be
thankful that he was safe. Yet still the pictures kept
flicking into her mind, fingers loosening and slipping
from a snapped off length of mast, waves washing over
closed eyes ... Oh God, anything but that. Even
Laverne ...

For some incomprehensible reason the mental comment made her giggle, then brought a sting of tears which took seconds to control. I must not be an idiot, she admonished herself with some severity, accelerating up the narrow road like a bat out of hell.

But two weeks later she had finally come to terms with the situation. So she told herself. Life still offered little pleasure but at least it was tolerable. She was even able to pretend to herself that she was forgetting Gray Ellison, that he was little more than a tarnished thread in the tapestry of her life. She refused to acknowledge the nights when she woke calling his name and with his picture so strong in her mind that she was shocked when she stretched out a hand to find he wasn't there. She never cried then but would lie for hours gazing into the darkness, wondering if the life that lay ahead of her was as empty and meaningless as the present moment. There were even a few occasions when she had resorted to one of the sleeping pills which had been prescribed by her doctor as a panacea for a broken engagement.

Besides, she remonstrated with herself in the mornings, if Laverne O'Casey was to his taste then let them enjoy each other. After all, what was he to her but part of her murky past? Come to think of it, she ought to be grateful to him that she had one and that was positively the very last thought she was going to have on the subject of Gray Ellison.

Her preparations for her evening with Anita and David were extensive for although she hardly cared to admit it, his opinion that she had lost weight, in other words that she was looking peaky, had rankled. But her reflection just before she left the house assured her that she was beginning to regain her looks which at one time she imagined had gone for ever. Not that it had seemed to matter then.

But tonight, thanks largely to a new range of make-up she had bought in Harrods, there was a glow about her which would receive the keenest inspection and in her eyes there was a sparkle that had nothing to do with artifice. She was really looking forward to the evening out, her first without the protective presence of one or other of her parents and a quiet dinner *à trois* was exactly the gentle kind of breaking-in she wanted.

She found them more dressed up than she expected for such an informal occasion but she was pleased, for she had wondered if her own exquisite chiffon blouse was a bit much. Only she had been anxious to show it off to Anita.

As it happened she was peacocking in a floor-length kimono in vibrant shades of bronze and black, cunningly cut to make the least of the bulge in front and slim at the back so that from certain angles she hardly looked pregnant at all. 'I'm all right so long as I keep walking backwards,' she joked. 'But yours, Leone! Tell me, where do you find all those marvellous clothes?'

'This came from London.' Leone touched the high Edwardian neckline of the blouse, liking the way the frill seemed to force her to hold her chin high. And to complement the style she had arranged her hair on top of her head, carefully ensuring that it looked just the least bit precarious and with one or two escaping tendrils to help the illusion along. She was pleased with herself, the midi-length skirt in clinging jersey accentuated her slender shape and the deep rose pink toned beautifully with her blouse. She raised a hand to touch her hair, enjoyed the seductive glimpse of flesh tints through the material, admired the row of tiny buttons which decorated the deep cuffs. 'The only thing I don't like about it is these,' she held out her arm. 'It took me such ages to fasten them. I mustn't wait too late for it's going to take me so long to get into bed when I get back.'

Downstairs they heard a doorbell ring then the sound of David's footsteps crossing the hall floor. Leone turned to Anita with a raised eyebrow.

'Oh, there's only going to be four of us, Leone.' Without looking at her friend she hurried to the door. 'I hope you won't mind. I didn't feel like coping with a big number tonight. In fact,' she put a hand to the small of her back and grimaced, 'I've had a terrible dragging pain all afternoon.'

'Oh, Anita.' At once Leone was all concern. 'If you weren't feeling like it you should have told me. I wouldn't have minded if you had wanted to cancel.'

'No, of course I didn't. I'm just explaining. I've been looking forward all week to this. Besides, Ellen did the cooking and she's come in tonight to help with the serving. I just told her what I wanted and as you know she's a far better cook than I am or ever likely to be. Anyway, so long as you're not disappointed. I would have liked to have had a crowd for your coming-out-again party but . . .'

Leone gave a delicate little shudder. 'I'm not. In fact I thought it would just be the three of us.'

'Oh.' Anita was making her way downstairs, Leone by her side. 'It's just an old friend of David's.'

And for a ghastly second Leone had the idea of a plan being hatched to bring her and Simon back together again. This was before she remembered with a ragged little sigh of relief that of course Simon was in the West Indies with Janet Maine. Of course that was a piece of gossip which Anita probably hadn't heard yet, she was looking forward to the opportunity of passing it on.

CHAPTER EIGHT

THE sitting-room in the large Victorian house had an alcove at one end, a shape which had posed a few problems for Anita who had redecorated it soon after her marriage. She had chosen a soft lilac shade for the carpet, a colour which was taken up more strongly in the flowered chintz covering one settee and several armchairs. A second sofa, pulled close to the blazing log fire was in a grey cord material, matching the curtains which hung at the tall windows. The walls were covered in a boldly striped paper in shades of mauve and purple on a white background with the merest impression of green somewhere in the background. But in the alcove she had used a dark glossy paper, almost black but in fact a very dark green, daring and dramatic and effective which, as she said, provided a perfect foil for David's growing collection of miniatures.

And that was apparently what was occupying the attention of her host and his visitor now for when they went inside the room appeared to be empty although there was a murmur of voices which registered just as Leone was smoothing her skirts in preparation to sitting. 'What a glorious fire,' she complimented her hostess, 'I love . . .' But behind Anita's head the two men moved into vision and her voice faded.

David was there but he didn't even register. The fact was she was dreaming again, she wasn't really here with Anita and David but in bed at home and soon she would wake up. And *he* would disappear. She blinked once, twice, but the face, dark, sardonic, stubborn as ever swam in front of her eyes, refused to go away. The features of the man she had sworn she would never see again . . . David was saying something but try as she might it was impossible for her to wrench her eyes away.

'. . . had no idea you'd met . . . haven't seen Gray for years . . . met him by chance in Weymouth this morning . . . hasn't met Anita before . . . persuaded him to come tonight.' Snatches of conversation penetrated into her shocked mind. '. . . mentioned your name and he said he knew you . . . Of course, I realise now you must have met.' He carefully avoided naming Simon and Leone heard the sound of her own voice with a casual greeting, neither enthusiasm nor the blank terror she was feeling showing through.

'Hello.' She didn't offer her hand and his fingers remained in the pocket of his dinner jacket, only the thumb showing. It was a little characteristic she had treasured for a brief period, one which caught at her heart even now. 'I didn't expect to see you.' Her voice was light, controlled and perfectly designed although she didn't realise it, for the role she had chosen to adopt at their last meeting.

'Nor I you.' His manner was equally smooth but still there was a tightness about his mouth which she couldn't explain. 'How are you?' The dark eyes were watching for the faintest betrayal and to her dismay she felt a tell-tale warmth in her cheeks. Of course, last time they met she had told him she was setting a date for her wedding. Now she didn't have even an engagement ring to help her out.

'Oh, I'm fine.' Her head was held high but that was probably due entirely to her high collar. 'And how were the Azores?' How ridiculous she sounded, as if she had escaped from an old Noel Coward play.

Before he had time to reply to that particularly

brilliant query, Anita had dropped into one of the chairs and was encouraging everyone else to follow suit. 'Just my luck,' she leaned her head against the back of her chair and Leone saw her hand going again to support her back, 'to look like this when meeting you for the first time, Gray. Yes, darling,' she responded to her husband's offer of a drink, 'only a fruit juice. That's another of the penalties, Leone,' she went on when they had all been supplied with drinks, 'alcohol is out for the whole of the nine months.'

'Never mind, Anita,' David perched himself on the arm of his wife's chair and patted her shoulder, 'when you go into hospital I'm going to appear with the biggest bottle of champagne you've ever seen.'

'When is your baby due?' Gray had obviously lost interest in Leone for now his hostess had all his attention. He turned on his charm and it was amusing to sit back and watch Anita respond with vivacity. Amusing and unexpectedly painful. Over the past weeks she had thought there was little she could learn about pain but now she was realising how wrong she had been. Sitting here now, watching him flirt just a little with an imminently pregnant woman in the presence of the husband, she was subject to even more violently tearing jealousy than she had experienced each time she thought of Laverne O'Casey.

'Tell me, Leone . . .'

She had hardly noticed David leave his perch on his wife's chair and join her on the sofa.

'How are you feeling, love?' And she transferred her attention to him with gratitude tinged with relief.

'I'm fine, David. Thanks.' Deliberately she kept her voice down so it was unlikely that Gray, immersed in his conversation with Anita, would be able to overhear, even if he wanted to. It was inevitable that he had asked about her marriage and would certainly know that it had been cancelled. So, the thought inflamed her feelings against him, feelings which the very sight of him had been in danger of softening, he was bound to think his efforts had achieved all the success he could have wished. And more.

For her dinner party Anita had chosen to seat her guests at a small round table, 'much more intimate' as she told them with a laugh as Ellen brought in the first course, than the long one they used for more formal occasions. So intimate indeed, Leone blushed at the unhappy choice of words, that Leone was forced to keep her feet firmly crossed beneath her chair lest by any chance her foot should encounter his. So intimate that each time she raised her head she encountered his dark expressive features which told her he knew of her embarrassment and was amused by it. Most of the time she tried to concentrate on what was being said by Anita or David but it was so artificial keeping her head at right angles that in the end she gave it up. And found a certain pleasure in the opportunities afforded by the position.

Much of the conversation centred on his recent trip to the Azores, interrupted by a flight to New York where he applied for patent papers for his most recent development. 'It looks like being successful.' Frowning he looked down and as he tapped the end of his cigar against the ashtray, Leone felt another pang of grief as she saw the dark crescent of lashes against his cheek. Then, quite suddenly, he looked up at her and the expression she saw increased the tempo of her breathing, moderated the pain to something softer, sweeter, infinitely more desirable. It was as if their minds were exchanging recollections of precious moments together, there was a suggestion in his dark eyes of desolation which was a shared experience. Yet, they contained a hint of accusation too . . .

Just then Ellen came into the room offering more coffee and she smiled as she listened to all their compliments about the meal which had been delicious.

'Thank you, Ellen. And you can go now if you want. Mr Shedden and I can do the coffee cups later on.'

'Are you sure, Mrs Shedden? I can easily wait.'

'No, I know you have visitors and you're anxious to be off.'

Leone had decided she would leave at a fairly early hour and she was taking her first glance at her watch when she thought she heard a little protest from Anita who was sitting on the settee beside her. She had been a bit concerned about her friend for in spite of all efforts she had been looking extremely strained and tired all evening and had eaten hardly any of the tempting food Ellen had taken such care over.

The men were engaged in conversation and she took advantage of that to lean over and squeeze Anita's hand. 'You all right?' she enquired softly.

'Fine,' Anita said but there was a film of perspiration on her upper lip, eyebrows were drawn together in a grimace of pain. 'It's just that I think I must have eaten something at lunch that disagreed with me. I've got a touch of indigestion now as well as backache.' She wrinkled her nose and tried, not very successfully to smile. 'The wages of sin,' she whispered.

Leone grinned and pushed herself forward to the edge of her seat. 'Well, I'm sure you're tired, Anita and I think I ought to be off.' She directed her remarks towards Gray Ellison and hoped he would take the hint. 'You'll be glad to get to bed I know but thank you for a lovely evening.' She got to her feet and a moment later David was standing beside her, looking down at his wife with some concern.

'Are you all right, darling?'

Anita nodded, began to murmur some reassuring platitude and took the hand her husband was offering to help her to her feet. Then her face contorted with pain, a groan refused to be stifled and that was almost immediately followed by a scream.

'Oh, David, I'm so sorry but I think . . .'

'Take it easy, darling.' David pushed her gently back into her seat. 'I'm going to get the car to take you to hospital.' He dropped a kiss on top of her head. 'Do you think this is it?'

Anita nodded, bit her lip and looked up with an attempted joke. 'I really don't think I can do anything much to delay it.'

'Don't even try. Look, Leone will sit and hold your hand till I get the car round.'

'Thanks, darling.'

When he had gone, Anita lay back and looked at her guests with a woebegone expression. 'What a thing to do to your guests at a dinner party.'

'Never mind.' Gray had sat down on the arm of the settee and took Anita's other hand. 'Most dinner parties we forget, this is one you've made certain will be forever imprinted on our minds.'

'Oh . . .' Anita closed her eyes as another pain seized her. 'Oh, I forgot about Davey. He's asleep and . . .'

'Don't worry about that.' Leone was reassuring. 'I'll wait till David gets back and . . .'

'But maybe he won't be back till morning. He wants to wait with me you see . . .'

'That's all right. I'll ring home and tell them that I'm going to stay the night. There's nothing at all for you to worry about. Now, what about your things? Shall I get them for you?'

'If you would, Leone. The case in the cupboard in the room where you left your coat. And that bed's made up. You can sleep there if you *do* have to stay the night. Although ... the way I feel ...' Leone was running up the stair by then and was relieved when she heard David open the front door and cross the hallway.

It wasn't until she had closed the heavy wood door behind them that she had time to realise that the situation as it had developed left her alone with Gray Ellison. It was something she would have run miles from if it could have been foreseen and one which she was determined should not be prolonged. So when she turned to him she made that plain enough.

'Well, I imagine you'll want to be on your way.' It was impossible to put it more forcefully than that, much as she would have liked to.

'Not at all.' He was looking at her with a hard stare that was all she needed to remind her of his character. His eyes were narrowed and even as she watched him, he took a case from his pocket, extracted a cigarette and lit it. The action made her aware of how badly she needed one herself to calm her shattered nerves and emotions. 'Anita asked me to stay here and keep you company.'

'I don't want any company.' She stalked past him into the sitting room and as a pointer to his bad manners she got a cigarette from her handbag and lit it, blowing the smoke sideways in an impatient little puff. That felt better.

'Nevertheless,' he threw himself down on the seat he had been occupying earlier and surveyed her through a haze of smoke, 'I feel bound by my promise to Anita.'

'How gallant,' she sneered. 'Maybe the best thing would be for me to go and leave you here babysitting. It doesn't take two of us to look after one small boy, especially when he's asleep.'

'But then if he wakes and finds a stranger here he

would be bound to feel alarmed. No,' suddenly he grinned, reminding her of the devastating effect of white teeth against his brown skin, 'I think we're stuck with each other, Leone, for tonight at least.'

She was about to demand what he meant by that remark when she changed her mind, and just as suddenly she lost her taste for the cigarette she was smoking and ground it out.

'That's better,' he approved, with a lazy watchfulness as she sat opposite him. 'Smoking really doesn't suit you.' He followed her example by stubbing out his own. 'I didn't know you had acquired the habit.'

Leone refused to look at him or answer, concentrating her attention on one of her shoes which she admired with absorbed interest.

'Leone.' She jumped when she realised he was standing in front of her and that he had spoken her name with barely concealed impatience. 'Look at me, damn you.'

For a second she thought of refusing but either his will was more powerful than hers, or more likely, she just liked looking at him. Even like this, dark eyebrows pulled together in anger, lips a hard relentless gash in his face, even then he was worth looking at. She tried to maintain an expression of cold distaste but she feared the soft yearning would show through, that he would sense, maybe even exploit, the overwhelming weakness she was incapable of mastering.

'Yes?' She drawled the word, hoping the cold, bored contempt would get under his thick skin. And it did, although the result was not the one she had hoped for although it should not have been a surprise when she was almost immediately wrenched to her feet.

'Don't try me too far, I might just lose my patience.'

'And what!' Her first shock was beginning to abate

although her heart was still hammering in wild agitation. And excitement. One small detached part of her psyche registered that fact, the adrenalin was pumping wildly through her veins, she was stimulated by the sudden acceleration in their dialogue, determined that this time at least she would not be the loser. 'What right have you either to keep or lose your temper with me? And why should I care in either case?'

'You *should* care.' His hands were on her shoulders, burning through the delicate material of her blouse as he gave her a little shake. She felt the agitated rise and fall of her breast, saw his attention drawn to the firm swell then move back to her face.

Then, quite suddenly all the emotion seemed to leave him and in some strange fashion she was left feeling deprived, bereft almost. His hands dropped to his side and she had an urge to take them in hers, to replace them or ... her mind wandered, eyes grew moist and dreamy with the yearning ... or to put them round her waist, hold them against her breast where he could feel the effect his presence had on her. But he had moved away from her, denying that impression she had picked up at some time during the evening that he, too, was suffering ...

'Tell me, Leone, what happened to you and Simon? I quite expected when I came back to hear that you were enjoying yourselves in some exotic honeymoon spot.' There was amusement in his voice, it didn't quite reach his eyes but she was too numb to interpret all the signs and found herself unwilling to answer his question. Throughout the evening she had been expecting some kind of interrogation, yet now it had come she found herself totally unprepared. 'Last time I saw you,' he paused, cruelly giving her time to remember all that had been said then, 'I was given to understand that you could hardly wait to arrange, rearrange rather, all the plans you had for your wedding to Simon Darcy. Don't tell me,' now the sarcasm was even more blatant, 'he changed his mind at the last minute.'

'Would that surprise you?' She was goaded into the remark. 'Isn't that what you *planned* for?' Then she bit her lip savagely.

'Are you telling me that's what *did* happen?' She was conscious of his close attention but she would not, *would* not look at him, only keeping him in sight at the very outer rim of her vision. Besides, if she did raise her eyes to his she was afraid she would show the tears quivering on her lashes. 'Leone,' his words began to force themselves through her disturbed emotions, 'is that what happened? Did Simon back out of the engagement?'

Then the enormity of what he was suggesting hit her, her pride reeled with shock and for a moment she experienced a little of what Mrs Darcy had made such a fuss about 'Of course he didn't,' she snapped and her anger had the effect of driving the tears away. 'Why do men always imagine that they are reluctant while women are over-eager? You all do it but you're usually wrong. Have you got that?' She whirled away from him, out of the room and without quite knowing what she was about she marched into the dining-room and began putting the dirty crockery on to a tray. 'Women are just as unwilling to give up their freedom as men are. And if you don't mind, I'm going to do the washing-up.'

By the time she had reached the kitchen and was swishing water in the bowl with an angry gesture Leone was feeling ridiculous. Especially as Gray had followed her through and even now was putting the coffee pot down on to the draining board. From the corner of her eye she could see a smile on his face, an expression that made her want to throw the wet dishcloth in his direction and at the same time tempted her to giggle.

'Here, I think you'd best let me wash, you can dry.' Automatically she accepted the towel he offered her, then pain stabbed through her as she remembered this was how they had always ended their meals on the *Sea Trekker*. And after that . . . her lips trembled.

Now instead of attending to the dishes Gray seemed to be fiddling with the sleeves of her blouse, where they had been splashed with washing-up water. 'Or you're going to spoil that pretty blouse. Have I told you that you're looking absolutely gorgeous tonight?'

'Wh . . . what?' She couldn't believe what he was saying. She must be imagining . . . But if she wasn't, then what better than to hear him repeating what she *thought* she had heard. 'What did you say?'

'Darling,' his voice sent shivers down her spine, 'I've been trying to tell you that since you came into the room this evening. You look gorgeous, enchanting.' His hand touched her hair, rested lightly against her cheek and his voice deepened, as if he were in the grip of emotions he could hardly control. 'You looked just as I have been telling myself for the last two months that you didn't look, gorgeous, enchanting and utterly . . . utterly irresistible.'

His mouth just touched hers, left her yearning for a more intense and prolonged contact but his lips were moving now, making sounds which gave her almost as much pleasure as his kiss.

'I've been in Hell since I saw you last. Cursing myself for not taking you off by force, for leaving you for Simon Darcy to enjoy for the rest of his life. When all the time I knew, had known from the first minute I set eyes on you, that I wanted you for myself, to be with me, to love desperately always.' He held her hands, looking at her as if he could spend the remaining days of his life doing nothing else and then, with a little moan, he gathered her to him, his hands moulding her so she felt the contours of his body absorb hers and his mouth fulfilling all the promises that his eyes and voice had been making.

'Leone.' He looked into her eyes, brilliant with happiness, then with another groan, he swept her up in his arms and carried her back to the sitting-room, depositing her gently on the large settee closest to the fire. 'You've put me through Hell.' Forgivingly he held her fingers against his cheek then took them away and pressed his lips against her open palm, smiling with a hint of triumph. 'But I told you that already, didn't I? Tell me,' he frowned as if he were having difficulty remembering, 'what did you say, something about my having planned your broken engagement? What on earth did that mean?'

By then Leone too was having problems in recalling exactly what she *had* said and even when her memory was totally clear, all those things she had held against him seemed to matter less and less.

'You . . . you had always been against our marriage hadn't you?'

'Had I?' He raised a surprised eyebrow. 'I don't remember having any feelings about it at all. You are talking about your marriage to Simon, I presume.'

'But you did. You had.' Now it was important for her to justify herself. 'You know you had. You had always said marriage was only for women and when Simon wrote to you about our engagement you sent that cable to him.'

For a second he stared in bewilderment then grimaced, shook his head and laughed briefly. 'Oh that. It wasn't meant to be taken seriously. It went back to our days in Cambridge when we thought we knew it all. We all promised each other that when one of us showed signs of doing something particularly stupid like say climbing the Eiffel Tower or getting married, then the rest of us would do our best to put the erring feet back on the straight and narrow. That's the only reason I sent the cable. It was meant to be a joke, for goodness sake, to remind him of the arrogance of youthful undergraduates. Besides, why should I worry whether Simon Darcy married, I was never all that friendly with him.'

'Well, you could have fooled me. From the way he spoke you and he were inseparable from the first day you met at school.'

'That's not how I remember it.' He frowned. 'There was quite a bunch of us, Simon was probably always on the fringe. Not one of my firmest friends although I did see more of him when we went up to Cambridge.'

'Well, he spoke so much about you that I got bored by the sound of your name and . . .'

'And . . .' he interrupted while he trailed a distracting finger down her throat, '. . . it didn't take you long to get over that, I seem to remember.' He grinned as the swift colour ran up under her skin then as his hand touched the curve of her breast she felt the wildfire begin to course through her veins. 'Didn't you?' he whispered insistently against her cheek.

'Yes. Oh yes.'

'So tell me, Leone,' his voice was as persuasive as she had ever known it, 'why did you run away from me as you did?'

'Run away?' It seemed so unlikely, so impossible that for a moment she was about to protest her innocence. But then, 'Oh that. It was something Laverne said. Laverne O'Casey.' She explained as if there were more than one.

'I know who Laverne is, for God's sake.' There was a return of the impatience that she knew was part of his make-up and which she'd better get used to, although this time she knew she was not its object. 'But what I want to know is what she said to make you bale out the way you did?'

'Oh, you know,' she shrugged, trying to avoid the searching eyes so close to hers, 'she gave the impression that you had asked me to go with you just to get me away from Simon. So that he would break the engagement.'

'She *what*?' He lifted himself away from her, his face a study in disbelief. 'Laverne told you *what*?'

'Oh, she didn't exactly *tell* me, but I overheard her speaking to Jeanette and that was what she said. I'm sure I didn't misunderstand. She said that you had told her and Lars that you could stop the wedding. And that one way of doing it was to make me fall in love with you.'

For some reason he ignored the first part of her explanation and concentrated on the last. 'And did it have that effect, Leone?' A tender hand touched her cheek. 'Is that what really happened? Did you fall in love with me?'

'Of *course* I did.' Indignation that he should doubt it made her eyes flash angrily. 'Do you think that I would have gone off with just anyone and . . .' Colour raced into her cheeks, she stopped speaking and bit her lip.

'And,' he spoke softly as if there were some danger of their being overheard, 'let me make love to you.'

'No.' Her lashes were lowered and she was unwilling to look up into his face, instead she watched her fingers toy with one of the buttons at her wrists. 'No, that wouldn't have happened if I hadn't fallen in love with you. No matter,' she flared suddenly and her lashes flicked back automatically, 'how carefully you planned the seduction.'

'Darling. Hush. Now let me tell you this and I hope you're going to believe me. There *was* some talk one night when we were on our way back from South Africa but it was just a lot of light-hearted banter. Incidentally, it was Laverne as I remember who made that particularly stupid suggestion. No matter what you think, I'm not quite as conceited as to imagine that I could have broken you up, even if I had wanted to. And I certainly didn't. Not then at least. Not till I saw you and then . . . you became an obsession with me.'

'Oh?' Her voice was faint and weak but that had much to do with the closeness of his mouth and it was some time before they returned to the theme which had such interest for both of them. 'Tell me about Laverne?' It was like rubbing salt into a sore but she wanted to get it out of the way. She would be as jealous as possible and then dismiss her from her mind.

'I told you.' His voice was blurry because he was kissing her throat. 'I told you she was the cook on board.'

'But there was something about the way you said it . . .' She caught hold of the hands which were determined to divert her from the conversation. 'As if . . . she might be something else . . . as well.'

'Oh, that?' He looked into her face and grinned. 'I was hoping you might be jealous. But, truly, as far as I was concerned that's all she was.'

'As far as you were concerned but she . . .'

'Will it satisfy you if I say that she and Lars have been together for a couple of years off and on? The only reason she got the job as cook was so she could be with him on the trip. But she's an amoral little thing and turns me off completely.'

'But she didn't turn you off that day when you got back from the Azores.' The words, uttered in a hurried sobbing voice were out before she could stop them. She held her breath then as she saw his eyes narrow.

'You ...' He was clearly trying to work something out. 'You were there ... when we got back?'

'Yes.' She hung her head guiltily. 'I had met her and she said the *Trekker* was overdue and I ... could hardly keep away from the harbour.' Recollection caused her lower lip to tremble, she caught it between her teeth 'I saw you ... with her and ...'

'You little idiot.' He smiled, shook his head disapprovingly. 'Why in heaven's name didn't you wait. It's true I gave her a hug when I reached the quayside but I would have hugged Sister ... what's her name ... Sister Maine if she had happened to be waiting there after our trip. It was just the least bit hairy. Now, that's positively my last word on the subject of Laverne O'Casey. If there's one thing I don't want it's a suspicious wife.'

'Wife?' For some reason that was the last word she had expected to hear and yet ... 'Do you mean ...?' she prompted almost coyly.

'I mean,' he looked down threateningly, 'I could break your neck when I think of the time we've wasted. Do you realise we could have been married as soon as we got back from Jersey? We could have had a wonderful time in the Azores, instead of which I was driven mad thinking of you with Simon. Him, above all people.' He paused briefly then went on, 'I've got a bit of a grudge against him. You see, he had an affair with my sister years ago and he made her very unhappy. At the time I didn't know who the man was, just that she was miserable. But it all came out just before I left South Africa, sparked off by his letter telling me of the engagement. She gave me a message for him, more or less saying that she no longer had any hard feelings and that she hoped he would be as happy as she now is. That's how I found out and I meant when I ran him to ground to let him know what I thought about him but of course when you find a man trussed up on a hospital bed it isn't so easy to be totally frank.'

'Oh?' A rather unpleasant thought had just occurred to her. 'I don't suppose it ever occurred to you that maybe . . .' to soften the pain her words might cause, she disengaged one of her hands from his and slipped it inside the front of his shirt, but then the pleasure she felt almost prevented her from going on, '. . . that maybe,' she moistened her lips with the tip of her tongue, 'you had hit on a . . . pretty nice way of getting your own back. For your sister, I mean.'

'Pretty nice,' his breathing had increased and he was regarding her through half-closed eyelids, 'is that how you would describe . . . what we did?'

'Pretty nice,' she agreed, moving her fingers over the warm skin. 'Sensational. Mind-bending. Anything you like.'

'No, at the time it didn't occur to me in those terms but later, when I was in the Azores and I was trying to find a proper stick to beat you both with, then that did come into my mind. But I couldn't convince myself. For I knew that all I wanted was to have you. The thought of him making love to you was . . . soul-destroying. For that there were no compensations. The only little one I could think of was that you weren't in love with him. But in that case why on earth were you determined to marry him?'

'You know . . .' her voice shook a little, '. . . if it hadn't been for his accident I had been going to call off the wedding. Each day that brought it nearer I was growing more and more panicky and I prayed for something to happen to stop it. I was sorry my prayers were answered the way they were but if it hadn't been for that I'm sure I would have broken my own leg just to give myself a breathing space. It was all a mistake from the beginning and I can't think how it happened.'

'Well, this time there's going to be no mistake. I'm going to see your father tomorrow and ask him if he minds if we get married at once. I hope he doesn't.' He grinned suddenly, so her heart gave a little skip of delight. 'For I'd hate to go against him.'

'I think they'll be very surprised but . . . maybe I can talk them both round. It'll have to be a pretty quiet affair, after the last time . . .'

'It shall be as quiet as you like.' He kissed her lingeringly. 'So long as it's at once. Speaking of which,' he surveyed her flushed cheeks with interset, 'did Anita mention something about a bed?'

'Oh, darling, we can't.' But her heart was bounding at the prospect. 'I . . .'

'I wasn't suggesting *that*. I was thinking that maybe you want to get there. Besides, I'm trying to be firm and wait till you've got my ring on your finger. A penance for past misdeeds. And I *did* worry about you. I had little else to do on the journey across the Atlantic. And I wondered if you had been telling me the truth about being on the pill and . . .'

'I didn't *say* that.'

'You implied it. Was it true, Leone?'

Unable to look him in the face she shook her head. 'No. You see, there was no point when I knew I wasn't going to marry Simon. And I had not intended to allow myself to be seduced by you.'

'You could have fooled me.' He laughed briefly then his face sobered all at once. 'Darling. The risks.'

'I know. My blood ran cold every time I thought of it. But luck was on our side.'

'No more risks then. Not till after the ceremony and even then, I want to have you to myself for a bit. I'm a selfish brute but it's only because I'm so crazy about you.'

'Oh, Gray ...' She shuddered. 'If you hadn't bumped into David today, what would you have done?'

'Oh,' idly he rubbed his chin against her cheek, 'I would have had to think of something else.'

It was a moment before the significance of his words penetrated her feelings of delicious euphoria, she jerked away from him, studying his face with a bewildered frown. 'What ... on earth do you mean?'

'I mean, my darling, that I was so desperate for news of you I *made* myself drop into David's office in Weymouth and tactfully, at least that was my intention, led the conversation round to Simon. That was when I first heard that the wedding still hadn't taken place. David gave me a couple of funny looks which reminded me I was sitting there with a stupid smile on my face, not really the expression one's expected to adopt on hearing such news. From there it was just a step towards wangling an invitation for this evening.'

'You wretch. So you knew you were going to see me. I,' she tapped him reprovingly on the chest, 'got the shock of my life when you walked out of that alcove.'

'I thought I had made a terrible mistake, that poisonous look you gave me ...'

'That was no more than you deserved. Of all the devious ...'

'And I arranged for Anita to go into labour as well. Just so we could have a little time to lie together like this ...' The arms holding her tightened.

'Mmm.' Instead of continuing the argument she chose to let her eyelids droop, to brush her lips provocatively against his in a way that almost instantly brought a very satisfactory response, made them lose all sense of time or place.

It was the slamming of a car door that brought them skimming back to earth where they landed with a bump and they were just separating when the front door closed, rapid footsteps crossed the hallway in the direction of the sitting-room.

'Just wait exactly where you are for the moment.' David poked his head inside the door then withdrew leaving the pair inside, sitting sedately facing each other from opposite sides of the fireplace, smiling rather foolishly.

David returned just a few minutes later, carrying a silver tray on which were three flute-shaped glasses and a bottle of champagne which he opened with a small flourish.

'Now,' he said, looking at each of them in turn, not troubling to hide the pleasure he was finding at prolonging their curiosity, 'I would like to propose a toast to my wife and new daughter.' Leone's smile expressed her satisfaction. 'To Anita and Natasha Leone.'

When the excited congratulations had died down and David had tried to answer all the queries about weight and colour of hair and eyes which Leone threw at him, they collapsed on to chairs while they discussed all the drama of the evening.

'It's not over yet.' Gray left his seat and came to perch on the arm of Leone's chair while David, insisting that it would be a shame to spoil the rest of the wine, refilled their glasses. 'Now Leone and I have some news for *you*.' She looked up at him with eyes that were brilliant with happiness and waited for him to speak the words which would confirm she hadn't just been dreaming.

The wedding which took place just two weeks later was as different from the first as it was possible to arrange. No large marquee in the garden of Clarewood, no choirboys, no cathedral church overflowing with rich and famous guests. It was true Lady Chevenix was just a bit sorry at being deprived of the great show she had always imagined and planned for her only child but she appeared to find considerable consolation in the strength and character of the man she was going to marry.

'It's strange,' she would say to whoever was listening, 'I felt there was something special about Gray the very first time we met. You remember how annoyed I was with Simon for arranging it? And yet it's all turned out so wonderfully well and even Meggy can't say anything since Simon went off with that nurse. I hear they spend all their time together now . . . And it's so obvious that Leone's in love.' Here she would sigh longingly. 'And I can't say I blame her.'

The bride, like her friend before her, had superstitiously decided against wearing white, choosing instead an Edwardian dress in deep cream-coloured lace, its long figure-hugging style suiting Leone's slender shape beautifully and the tiny swathed chiffon apron making a perfect foil for her posy of tea roses. In her hair she wore roses too, a bandeau of pale yellow buds interlaced with glossy leaves. She had never looked lovelier, her father decided as they stood together in the porch of the village church. And yet her appearance had more to do with the glow of happiness in her eyes than with the sumptuous dress she was wearing. With that look of trembling, expectant, unquenchable joy she would have been stunning in sackcloth.

'Ready, Leone?' He gave her an encouraging smile as the verger pushed open the heavy door for them.

She nodded, her eyes blurred with sudden tears. 'I'm ready.' Standing on tiptoe she touched her lips to his cheek. 'And thank you, Daddy. You and Mummy have been marvellous.' She had to blink once or twice before she could go on. 'I've put you through it the last month or two, haven't I?'

He shook his head. 'Of course you haven't.' It was a tiny lie which deceived them both in their present mood of almost total happiness. 'It's only in the last two weeks I've realised just how wrong things were last time. This time, no mistakes.'

No, this time, no mistakes. That certainty swelled in her breast as slowly she walked up the aisle, the sounds of the wedding march in her ears played with all the *fortissimo* the organist could obtain from his wheezy instrument. Then, as she reached the tall, dark-clad figure he turned, swept her with a possessive look before reaching out to clasp her hand, together they kneeled at the altar rail in front of the clergyman.

'Dearly beloved, we are gathered here today . . .'

The pressure on her fingers increased, his thumb found a sensitive spot and stroked tantalisingly. From beneath lowered lashes she sent a provocative glance which encountered one of his. The firm lips curved in the faintest of smiles, her heartbeats increased rapidly, she sighed imperceptibly from sheer joy.

This time there was no mistake.

 **Harlequin Romance**

Coming Next Month

2773 SHADOWS OF EDEN Rosemary Badger
Meeting a handsome wealthy author is just what the
survivor of an accident that claimed her family needed—
until her feelings turn to love and he starts to pull away.

2774 SAND CASTLES Meg Dominique
The manager of Florida's Hotel Fandango is ready to settle
down, while his ladylove doesn't dare stay in one place
long enough to get involved. Yet when he holds her in his
arms anything seems possible.

2775 AGE OF CONSENT Victoria Gordon
Despite the crush she once had on him, an out-of-work
journalist turns to a writer in Tasmania for help—only to
find that he and his beautiful girlfriend add to her worries.

2776 POWER POINT Rowan Kirby
A child psychologist puts her heart at risk when she breaks
all her rules of professional detachment in order to help a
dynamic documentary producer reach his young brother.

2777 BLUEBELLS ON THE HILL Barbara McMahon
In the peaceful Sierra Nevada, a rancher, still bitter over the
desertion of his wife, opens up to a woman who can't tell
him she isn't exactly what she seems.

2778 RETURN TO FARAWAY Valerie Parv
A film producer returns to the Australian Outback at her
estranged husband's invitation. Or so she thinks. But his
resentful teenage daughter from a previous marriage is up
to her old tricks!

Available in July wherever paperback books are sold, or
through Harlequin Reader Service.

In the U.S.
901 Fuhrmann Blvd.
P.O. Box 1397
Buffalo, N.Y. 14240-1397

In Canada
P.O. Box 2800, Postal Station A
5170 Yonge Street
Willowdale, Ontario M2N 6J3

Can you keep a secret?

You can keep this one plus 4 free novels

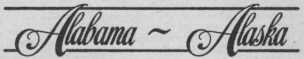

Harlequin "Super Celebration"
SWEEPSTAKES

NEW PRIZES—NEW PRIZE FEATURES & CHOICES—MONTHLY

1. To enter the sweepstakes, follow the instructions outlined on the Center Insert Card. Alternate means of entry, NO PURCHASE NECESSARY, you may also enter by mailing your name, address and birthday on a plain 3" x 5" piece of paper to: In U.S.A.: Harlequin "Super Celebration" Sweepstakes, P.O. Box 1867, Buffalo, N.Y. 14240-1867. In Canada: Harlequin "Super Celebration" Sweepstakes, P.O. Box 2800, 5170 Yonge Street, Postal Station A, Willowdale, Ontario M2N 6J3.

2. Winners will be selected in random drawings from all entries received. All prizes will be awarded. These prizes are in addition to any free gifts which might be offered. Versions of this sweepstakes with different prizes may appear in other presentations by TorStar and their affiliates. The maximum value of the prizes offered is $8,000.00. Winners selected will receive the prize offered from their prize package.

3. The selection of winners will be conducted under the supervision of Marden-Kane, an independent judging organization. By entering the sweepstakes, each entrant accepts and agrees to be bound by these rules and the decision of the judges which shall be final and binding. Odds of winning are dependent upon the total number of entries received. Taxes, if any, are the sole responsibility of the winners. Prizes are not transferable. This sweepstakes is scheduled to appear in Retail Outlets of Harlequin Books during the period of June 1986 to December 1986. All entries must be received by January 31st, 1987. The drawing will take place on or about March 1st, 1987 at the offices of Marden-Kane, Lake Success, New York. For Quebec (Canada) residents, any litigation regarding the running of this sweepstakes and the awarding of prizes must be submitted to La Regie de Lotteries et Course du Quebec.

4. This presentation offers the prizes as illustrated on the Center Insert Card.

5. This offer is open to residents of the U.S., and Canada, 18 years or older, except employees of TorStar, its affilliates, subsidiaries, Marden-Kane and all other agencies and persons connected with conducting this sweepstakes. All Federal, State and local laws apply. Void where prohibited or restricted by law. Winners will be notified by mail and may be required to execute an affidavit of eligibility and release which must be returned within 14 days after notification. Winners consent to the use of their name, photograph and/or likeness for advertising and publicity in conjunction with this and similar promotions without additional compensation. One prize per family or household. Canadian winners will be required to answer a skill testing question.

6. For a list of our most recent prize winners, send a stamped, self-addressed envelope to: WINNERS LIST, c/o Marden-Kane, P.O. Box 525, Sayreville, NJ 08872.

No Lucky Number needed to win!